DYE, DYEING, DEAD

A "Nameless, Texas"
Mystery Novella

*Featuring Kendra Louise Harper,
Texas Folklorist*

by Bobbi A. Chukran

Limestone Ledge Publishing
Taylor, Texas

First paperback edition: August 2014

ISBN # 978-0-944577-12-7

Cover art by Bobbi A. Chukran

Edited by Christina Gatti

For Rudy, as always

The first 25+ years have been an amazing journey. Let's do 25 more. And then some.

***

*For Dianne,
Best Little Sister in the World!
You are an inspiration.*

***

*For all my friends in the online communities –
thanks so much! I couldn't have done it without
you.*

CAST OF CHARACTERS

* Buddy Byers...owner of Buddy's Hardware Store & Sundry Sundries. Somebody went nuts on him with the tattoo gun
* Buster Briggs...gruff, no-nonsense good ol' boy county sheriff, likes pie
* Mrs. Eula-Mae Bunch...belligerent troublemaker and garden club president
* Flora Martin...mother of Oma and Alma Martin
* Pastor Garvey Holt...Pastor of the First Christian Baptist Free -Will Church
* Ginger Marshall...Kendra's friend, 30-ish, a local art-quilter
* Harry Bunch...Eula-Mae's son
* Jack Adams...AKA Mr. Magoo. Kendra's and Jewel's neighbor who says he witnessed the murder
* Jeremy Clifford...Kendra's best pal, late-20s, sidekick and partner in mayhem, theatrical, works at Do-Lolly's Diner in downtown Nameless
* Jewel Moore...60-something, Kendra's aunt/roommate, avid gardener, feisty
* Deputy Jim Wyman...Kendra's love interest, smitten with her
* Kendra Louise Harper...35-year old folklorist, author and sometimes sleuth, gardener

* Lolly LaRue…owner of Do-Lolly's Diner; sassy, middle-aged, wise
* Nora Rogers…Nameless librarian, early 40s, studious
* Oma and Alma Martin…owners of a small organic farm outside town, hippy gals
* Sarah Wilson…owner of Sarah's Needles & Threads, small downtown yarn shop
* Verna Holt…Pastor Holt's devout wife, fond of classic fashion
* Virginia Marshall…Ginger's 14-year-old daughter

CHAPTER ONE

The white-haired woman stooped over a rusty iron cauldron, stirring the boiling contents with a long, gnarled stick. Fire leapt from beneath it with a crackle and the smell of pungent pecan wood smoke filled the September air.

"More wood!" she demanded, brushing her hair back from her forehead with her wrist.

A small figure scurried to fulfill her wishes. Someone giggled then began to chant, in a low, soft voice. "Bubble, bubble toil and trouble, Fire burn and cauldron bubble."

"Ah ha!" the woman cackled, stirring a beaker of white powder into the boiling liquid. "We're almost ready."

The chanting continued. "Eye of newt and toe of frog . . ."

"What did you say? Eye of what? Is that like a lizard or something? Wait a minute. Where in the world do you buy newt's eyes? And who around here's fast enough to catch a frog and get his toes?"

"Yuck," another commented. "That's not just wrong; it's cruel."

"Hey, look, Miss Smarty Pants. I didn't write it, I just recite it. Listen to this part—wool of bat and tongue of dog."

"Wool of bat? Hmm. Now that's very interesting. How exactly do you gather the wool from a bat? Do you suppose you have to pluck it? Or shear it, like a sheep?"

"You'd have to use an incredibly small pair of clippers to shear a bat, don't you think?" another said. "Or tweezers? You could do it with tweezers, I bet. You'd have to pluck a bat."

"Yeah, right—like a bat is just gonna hang around and let you tweeze it."

The other nodded. "That would be a problem. I don't suppose you would get much wool, either. Wouldn't be worth the trouble."

"Nope," the group agreed.

"That's why the line says 'toil and trouble,' I bet."

"Yep," they agreed again.

"Maybe it's fur on a bat?"

The woman straightened up with a groan and clutched at her back. "Are y'all gonna stand around here all day practicing your comedy routine and quoting Billy Friggin' Shakespeare, or are you gonna help me get this plant workshop going?"

Kendra Louise Harper smiled at her aunt. "Of course we are, Aunt Jewel! We're just having a bit of fun, that's all."

Jewel Moore frowned at her niece. "Looks

8

like I'm doin' all the work while y'all flap your lips, makin' fun! Not to mention that it sounds like y'all had one-too-many margaritas for lunch, too."

Ginger Marshall giggled. "Who, us?"

"Sorry," Kendra mumbled, scrambling to take the stirring stick from her and taking her place beside the huge iron pot. Her aunt might be right about the margaritas. That new watermelon margarita recipe she'd tried was really good.

To tell the truth, Kendra silently wondered why she'd offered to help with the workshop considering how much of her own work she had to do. Ever since her Aunt Jewel started teaching gardening workshops at their house, her own life had been severely disturbed. She'd barely had time over the last few weeks to work on her own book, a collection of local ghost stories. Her deadline was rapidly approaching.

In general, at the age of 35, Kendra felt time sliding away from her. Kendra was a folklorist who had studied Texas legends and lore. She told people that folklore was one of those college degrees that doesn't take you very far unless you get a Ph.D. and end up teaching other people. Kendra didn't follow that path like most of her schoolmates did. She chose to do her own thing and went into independent research, and had a whole list of projects she wanted to tackle.

Luckily, her Aunt Jewel, a widow for three years, had come to the rescue when Kendra's five-year marriage ended. It didn't take much to convince Kendra to move to Nameless into Jewel's tiny 1940s cottage. Together, they remodeled the old house and after a period of re-adjustment, they fell into a nice routine.

Kendra felt that she and her aunt made swell housemates. They both loved gardening and maintaining the large corner lot. Aunt Jewel loved to bake and Kendra loved experimenting with all the herbs they grew. They both loved to eat and her friends loved sampling their efforts. An additional bonus was that Kendra had found Jewel's older friends to be very helpful in researching the local ghost stories. It was a win-win situation.

Now that she had settled into her new home, she was eager to delve into her work. She had one book almost finished and several others on the back burner. Kendra was anxious to hide away and write, but first, she had to keep her promise to help her aunt with this workshop.

The steam from the cauldron was thick and hot. Kendra blew out a breath and pushed her dark hair back out of her face and tried to tuck it back into the braid that lay down the middle of her back. It immediately sprung back, curling into her dark green eyes. Kendra made a mental note to get a haircut.

Her aunt had been planning this Dyeing with Plants workshop for over three months. The fall weather had turned out beautifully, the crisp blue sky filled with soft, billowy clouds. The humidity that was common year-round in Central Texas had been chased away by a cooling rain shower the night before. Kendra knew that it would be hot and humid again before the afternoon—probably near 100-degrees—if not higher. For now she was thankful for the (slightly) cooler weather.

Kendra's aunt was known for her gorgeous gardens where she mixed native plants with herbs and old-fashioned roses. They covered almost all of the large corner lot near downtown Nameless. Over the last few years, after Jewel had turned 60, she'd been bored and out-of-sorts, wondering what she'd do with the rest of her life. Not one to rest for long, she'd decided to start teaching local classes on gardening—how to design small gardens, how to use flowers and herbs in crafts and how to cook with herbs. From time to time, she also wrote a short garden column for the Nameless News.

Once she'd decided to give outdoor classes, Jewel and Kendra had spent months remodeling the large backyard shed into classroom space and putting a brick patio underneath a huge ancient pecan tree.

In addition to Kendra and a few of her friends, Aunt Jewel was expecting at least a dozen others for the workshop, mostly members of the Nameless Garden Club and a few of Kendra's friends from town.

Aunt Jewel's workshops were always popular and they filled quickly. For one thing, there wasn't a whole lot to do otherwise in Nameless, and artistic people were somewhat of a curiosity in the small town with a population of 2,354—give or take a few. The next closest center of cultural knowledge was Austin, and that was over 30-miles away.

There was one movie theatre in town that showed two movies at a time. It was only open on the weekends and showed one movie upstairs and one downstairs. Kendra still wasn't used to that after going to the multiplex theatres in Austin for so many years.

Jewel loved to share her garden with others, and show people how many ways the plants could be used. In an area where invasive nandina shrubs and non-native boxwoods lined up beside every other house on the block, Jewel's garden was different, and attracted all sorts of attention.

Luckily, the love of gardening had rubbed off on Kendra. She figured it was genetic. She remembered walking underneath okra plants when she was much younger and was sure that was why she was so interested in plant lore.

After Kendra moved away from Austin and moved in with her aunt, they had spent several years designing and cultivating a small themed dyer's garden around the perimeter of the back yard courtyard. Jewel used many of these plants for her workshops. She wasn't much of a fiber person, but did use the yarns she dyed in small knitting projects.

Jewel's prized indigo bush, from which she had plucked some of the leaves for today's workshop, stood proudly against the short rock wall dividing her property from her closest neighbor. Edging it was a whorl of prickly green leaves belonging to the madder plant—a plant whose roots produce a red dye that had also been used for centuries before synthetic dyes were discovered. Red, pink and salmon cosmos nodded in the wind and deep orange marigolds edged the paths.

Kendra glanced at her watch as members of the garden club walked through the front gate, chatting excitedly, smelling the roses and exclaiming over the garden. Although it was September, everything was blooming abundantly now, and Kendra thought it looked best at this time of year. She knew that early fall in Texas could be as scorching hot as the middle of the summer, sometimes hotter. The heady scent of the antique roses wafted on the breeze and bird song filled the air.

Kendra took a last look at the setup, making sure Jewel had all the equipment she needed. The contents of two large stainless steel pots simmered on hot plates that were plugged into the outlet on the back porch. Sacks of dried flower petals and huge branches of fresh rosemary sat to the side. A large jar of indigo sat underneath the worktable.

Kendra's friend, Ginger Marshall, a local art quilter, had volunteered to help since she was definitely into the whole fiber thing. Ginger was an internationally-known quilt artist that tended to do work that would never see the top of anyone's bed. Wall quilts, she called them. Jeremy Clifford, another friend, hovered nearby.

Kendra looked up to greet the group of women that had begun to gather. She suppressed a groan. They were dressed for a tea party, not a messy, drippy dye workshop. She had warned them to dress casually, but old habits were hard to break. This was an event in town, and the ladies of the Nameless Garden Club always dressed up for events. Some of them were even wearing white gloves. Did anyone do that anymore? Kendra wondered. The hats made sense; the sun could turn hot and deadly by noon—but gloves? She shook her head. What was this, church? They'd have to scrounge around and find aprons or old shirts for the women to slip over their clothes. Now that would be an amusing sight, Kendra thought.

"My, my, would you look at that?" Jeremy Clifford whispered. "What have we here, a Donna Reed reunion show?"

Kendra laughed. "Yeah, really. We'll have to find aprons for this bunch. Aunt Jewel will have a cow when she sees how they're dressed."

"You got that right," he said. Jeremy was one of the more artistic of Kendra's friends. He was an

14

avid member of the local community theatre group and worked at Do-Lolly's Diner in the mornings and whenever Lolly LaRue, the owner, needed him. He said it gave him material for the short plays he was trying to write.

Jeremy watched as the women trailed in. "I do love those gloves. And the hats! The hats are marvelous! I'll have to see if I can borrow some for our next production."

Jeremy was a fan of vintage women's clothing that he frequently wore in his productions at the local community theatre, a fledgling group of six intrepid souls who kept the group together. He was still glowing from his recent spectacular performance as ten of the characters in the Greater Tuna play. The Nameless News had reviewed the play and said that it was "a pure-dee delight and inspirational casting" putting Jeremy in the roles. He agreed. Of course, it helped that he was the producer and director.

"Hello, Kendra," a short, older lady said. Eula-Mae Bunch was the president of the Nameless Garden Club and involved in numerous community groups. "And hello, Jewel," she called to Kendra's aunt. She frowned at Jeremy. "I had no idea you would be here."

Kendra smiled sweetly, wiping her hands on the back of her jeans. "Mornin', Mrs. Bunch."

Jeremy bowed and smiled. "Mrs. Eula-Mae Bunch! I'm delighted to see you. Of course I'm

15

here to help Aunt Jewel whenever she needs me. I'm like part of the family. I'm surprised you're here, though, what with your busy schedule with the garden club, and the school board and the library committee and I don't know what all."

Kendra gave Jeremy the evil eye, but smiled.

Eula-Mae Bunch sniffed, tugging the cuffs of her white gloves firmly up her wrists. "Yes, I am terribly, terribly busy," she said, smiling at Kendra and ignoring Jeremy. "But not too busy to keep up with what our resident folklorist is doing these days. I trust you are working on something and keeping yourself busy, dear."

"Nosy old witch," Aunt Jewel murmured under her breath, turning to greet the rest of the group.

Kendra frowned at her aunt and rushed to take Mrs. Bunch's arm and lead her out of Aunt Jewel's way. The two women had never got along with each other, and she didn't want a scene in front of the other participants. "I've been extremely busy. I'm working on a collection of Texas ghost stories."

"Oh, is that so? Well, how interesting," Mrs. Bunch said as she tottered over to her chair.

Other members of the garden club spread through the garden, remarking on the copper labels that Kendra had used to mark the plants, and the handmade red birdhouse that perched on one corner of the garden fence.

Ginger scurried around, trying to set chairs out for the group and find aprons and old shirts to cover their clothes.

Alma and Oma Martin, twin sisters, drove up in their rusty Ford truck, clambered down out of the cab, then hung back at the gate, shyly whispering among themselves. The two sisters wore their long hair piled up on their heads, and long brightly embroidered cotton print dresses stretched almost to their ankles. They wore almost no make-up or jewelry, and each carried a large basket piled high with fluffy natural-color yarns. The Martins owned a small organic farm outside town.

"The hippy-dippy sisters are here," Jeremy whispered to Kendra.

"Hush!" she hissed, and moved to greet the sisters. She was a bit surprised to see them there. They rarely came to town unless it was a necessity.

Sarah Wilson, another of Kendra's friends and owner of Sarah's Needles and Threads, a small yarn, knitting and needlework shop in downtown Nameless, rushed to greet the two women.

"Hi! I was glad to hear that y'all were coming today. I'm sure you'll enjoy it. Jewel will be glad to see you." She peeked into the basket. "And you brought some of your lovely handspun yarn! Wonderful!"

Alma nodded at Sarah with a shy smile. "We don't get out much to socialize, what with taking

17

care of all the sheep and chickens and all." She held out her basket. "Kendra said we could bring this instead of paying our fee. We're really excited about the workshop. We've never tried using natural dyes on our yarns before. It's something we've always wanted to learn how to do. We sure appreciate you lettin' us sit in on it."

"No problem. Look, you're doing us a favor. We need all the yarn we can get today, so Jewel was glad to hear you were coming. Let me take those baskets from you and I'll go tell her you're here."

The two sisters handed the baskets over to Sarah then quietly took a seat at the picnic table to the side of the yard.

Mrs. Bunch marched up to the steaming iron cauldron and peered inside. "Huh. Looks like water to me," she sniffed, pulling back and waving her hand in front of her face as a puff of steam billowed up.

"It is water, Eula-Mae," Jewel explained. "Water with alum dissolved in it. We'll simmer the yarn in the pot before we dip it into the dyes."

"Alum? Isn't that something you use to make dill pickles?" Mrs. Bunch asked, wrinkling her nose.

"Yes, sometimes," Jewel answered. "I'll explain it all later when everyone gets here."

Eula-Mae sniffed and pointedly looked at her wristwatch. "You said we'd start promptly at 9:00, and it's 9:08 already. I do have quite a few other very important appointments today."

"Oh dear, of course. Why don't you try to relax and have a seat. We'll be starting shortly." Jewel looked over the crowd, counting heads. "Looks like almost everyone's here."

Just then a short, stout woman huffed up the driveway and slammed through the gate. Kendra winced as the old antique gate banged back against the wrought-iron fence that rimmed the front yard, crushing a climbing rose in her wake.

"I'm not late, am I?" Verna Holt trilled. "We had a prayer meetin' over at the church this mornin', and Pastor did go on and on and on. I hope y'all weren't holdin' everything up for me, were you? How sweet!" The woman was dressed for church, complete with a navy blue linen suit, straw hat and white gloves. A large red ribbon rose was perched on the back of the hat and long ribbons in the back fluttered in the breeze like paper streamers. "I did expect some of y'all to be there, however," she sniffed.

A few of the women pursed their lips, ducked their heads and looked the other way.

Coming right along behind Verna was Nora Rogers, head of the Nameless Public Library. She greeted several of the women as she passed, and smiled at Kendra as she took a chair towards the front of the audience. She looked around and made a sour face when she saw Eula-Mae.

Ginger looked at Kendra, trying to suppress a grin. "Looks like Mrs. Preacher is here."

"Yep. Looks like." She pursed her lips and mumbled. "Help me keep her away from Mrs. Bunch if at all possible, will ya?" she asked.

Kendra glanced at the pastor's wife, then Mrs. Bunch, then Aunt Jewel. The potential for disaster was great with this particular group of women in the same gathering. Volatile was the word that came to mind.

Even though she attended Verna's husband's church every Sunday, and every Wednesday night for prayer meeting, Eula-Mae Bunch had held a grudge against the pastor's wife for over ten years. No one really knew why, but rumor had it that it had something to do with Pastor Holt and his propensity to want to minister to the widows of Nameless. And if they should happen to give him a large donation for the church in the meantime, even better. He'd be able to pay the electric bill and they would get a nice donation to list on their income taxes.

"Now, if everyone would find a seat," Kendra called, "we'll get started." The clamor of voices finally died down. Kendra looked out on the group, excited for her aunt that so many had decided to attend.

As Kendra opened her mouth to speak, Mrs. Bunch jumped up and exclaimed, "The Nameless Garden Club is honored to be invited to your little talk. I think we can dispense with the usual business meeting beforehand, since this is such an unusual circumstance. I'm sure we'll all find the subject fascinating, don't you, girls?" She looked around at the group and several nodded and bobbed their heads in answer. No one ever dared contradict Eula-Mae Bunch.

She continued. "Although for the life of me, I can't see why anyone in these days and times would want to go to all this trouble."

"But I . . ." Jewel started.

"We use those easy dyes that come in a box on the choir robes over at the church when they start looking a little faded and ratty," Mrs. Holt interrupted. "I use it myself, sometimes," she confessed. "It's real easy. You can buy it in little boxes at the grocery store!"

"Also," Mrs. Bunch continued, ignoring the pastor's wife, "you can do down to Sarah Wilson's shop in town and buy simply scads of lovely yarns, already dyed." She smirked and glanced over at Sarah, who was hunkering down in her chair out of embarrassment.

Kendra gave Sarah a sympathetic smile, and tried once again to interrupt. "Mrs. Bunch, we really need to get started."

"Kendra, dear. Now please let me finish. Like I said, I'm sure we'll all enjoy ourselves nevertheless." She started to sit down, but popped back up. "But you do know, dear, don't you, that the commercial dyes are less prone to fade."

21

"Ah yes. So easy—but so unnatural," Jewel murmured, glaring at Eula-Mae, wondering why she had bothered to show up in the first place.

By now, Kendra was gritting her teeth so hard her forehead was puckered and she felt the beginnings of a headache coming on. "Yes, um . . . well. Ginger, if you will pass around these yarn samples, we'll get started."

As Ginger passed around samples of yarn, Kendra explained that all of them had been dyed with plants from their garden. Jewel showed the group the proper way to tie the yarn into a small skein so it wouldn't get tangled in the dye bath.

Kendra dipped a small white skein into a pan of warm water and let it soak for a few minutes. "The yarn has to be completely saturated with water so the dye will penetrate the fibers."

"Now, I want all of y'all to try it," Jewel announced. "Step up here and grab an apron or a shirt to put over your clothes. I have lots of yarn up here. We'll all tie a sample skein and put it in to soak for a while."

One by one, the group timidly rose to their feet, took the yarn pieces held out to them and proceeded to make small skeins. Mrs. Bunch remained in her chair, now and then pointedly looking at her watch.

"Wouldn't you like to try it?" Jeremy asked her.

Mrs. Bunch shook her head and wrinkled her nose as if he had suggested stroking a dead armadillo. "I don't think so. You all go ahead. I'll just sit here and observe."

Oma, Alma and Verna gingerly stepped up to the pot and peered in. The pastor's wife removed her gloves, tucking them in her purse. "I do hate wearing these, but Pastor insists. I'd hate to get them ruined; they're my only pair. And it's so hard to find nice white gloves anymore."

Jeremy nodded. "Boy, ain't that the truth!"

After all the skeins were tied and soaking in the water, Kendra explained how the yarns next had to be mordanted, or treated with the solution of alum water, so that the dyes would bond with the woolen fibers and be permanent. Jewel used alum because it was relatively non-toxic, unlike a lot of the other traditional metallic mordants. Using a long gnarled stick, she fished the skeins out of the warm water one-by-one, and dropped them into the large iron vat to simmer. Jewel explained how important it was to make sure the wool wasn't shocked by overly cold water.

While the yarn was simmering, Jewel passed around samples of the plants that had been used to make the dyes. She showed a sample of indigo leaves from her garden, natural indigo powder, and a hard rock-like pebble of synthetic indigo that had to be crushed with a hammer before using. She also passed around a section of madder root from their garden, a plant that would make a beautiful reddish-purple dye. Most of the members were

23

familiar with rosemary as a culinary herb, but didn't know it could be used as a dye plant, too.

Mrs. Bunch tottered to the front and peered into the pot. "Seems like all you're doing is washing yarn that's already clean," she said. "Is this going to take much longer? Is all this really necessary?" She glanced at her watch. "Kendra, dear, we really should be getting on with it."

Kendra tried to ignore her, and proceeded to demonstrate to the rest of the group the steps necessary for processing the plant materials so that the dye would be released. She explained that plant leaves could be boiled, but roots had to be macerated and smashed.

She dropped a large sack of dried marigold petals into a small pot of simmering water, and the group gathered around to watch. As the water turned from clear to a light yellow, then to a deep golden color, the group oohed and aahed in unison.

Kendra grinned in response. "This is why, Mrs. Bunch, we spend so much time doing this. It's fun!"

Mrs. Bunch sniffed and stood to the side with her arms crossed over her chest.

"Careful, this might splash," Jewel warned the group as she strained the water to remove the flower heads. "The dye will be different colors, depending on the variety of flower used, the acidity of the water, whether it was dried or fresh, and even when or where the plants were

24

harvested." She explained that summer flowers made different colors than spring flowers.

She showed them how to make other colors using madder root she had dug from their garden, fresh rosemary and another using dried onion skins.

One by one the women dropped their skeins into one of the dye baths and stood aside as the liquids simmered. When the colors were dark enough, Ginger fished them out, carefully rinsed, and hung them from Jewel's clothesline to dry.

The women were excited now, marveling and clucking over "their" skeins and trying to decide what they would make out of them once they took them home. Most of the women were sporadic knitters or crocheted a little.

"Now for a little magic," Jewel announced mysteriously.

The women took their seats again as Kendra reached under the table and carefully pulled out a two-gallon glass jar filled with a murky, dark liquid. Jewel explained that she had been using the liquid indigo in the same jar for several years.

"Indigo is a dyestuff that has been used for centuries. At least since 2500 B.C. You probably know it best as the dye in blue jeans. It is one of the few blue dyes that are naturally found in nature. Indigo doesn't dissolve in water so you have to add a chemical to change it temporarily to what is called 'indigo white' to get the leaves to release the blue pigment."

She sat the glass jar carefully in a shallow pan of warm water, opened up the top, and poured in sodium hydrosulfite. She explained how the chemical worked in the process. As the water began to heat, the liquid started turning a sickly yellowish-green color.

"The liquid has to turn to this color before we can use it as a dye. When we dip the yarn into the liquid, and bring it out again, it interacts with the air and turns into the traditional dark blue color we know as indigo."

Jewel dipped a small skein of yarn into the jar, waited a few minutes and pulled it back out. As soon as the yarn came in contact with the air, it began turning, almost magically, from the yellowish color to a deep, dark, indigo blue. "And if you want a darker color, let it dry, then repeat the process. Just keep dippin' it until it's as dark as you want."

"Oh, wow! Would you look at that?" Ginger exclaimed, clapping her hands.

"Cool. Really cool," Sarah commented. "I had no idea!"

"Humph! Really, Jewel, must you be so—so dramatic?" Eula-Mae Bunch said. "All this hocus-pocus. Is this really necessary? Is this what we came to see?"

Kendra stared at Mrs. Bunch, trying to keep calm. Why, the nerve of the old witch, talking to Aunt Jewel like that!

Ginger stood up, throwing Mrs. Bunch a withering glance. "I think it's time for a break. We have some refreshments ready, and we'll meet back here in about twenty minutes for the conclusion of the workshop."

Kendra gave her a grateful smile, as she took a deep breath and fought to keep her temper. She glanced at Jewel, who also looked like she wanted to spit nails. Kendra could tell she was NOT happy. And she didn't blame her. She'd spent a lot of time getting the workshop ready.

Ginger said, "If you ladies would be so kind to come around to the back porch, we have lavender cookies and hibiscus tea ready there for you. Just follow the stone pathway around the corner to the back garden area."

A smattering of applause broke out over the group, as the women rose from their seats, removing their smocks and aprons, pulling their gloves back on, adjusting their hats, clutching their purses to their bosoms, and tottering their way down the sidewalk, through the garden to the porch. They stopped here and there to exclaim over the heirloom roses that were putting on a fall show.

Kendra saw her aunt heading for Mrs. Bunch, full steam ahead. She reached out to stop her, but Jewel shrugged her off. "Let me be, Kendra. It's

27

about time someone told off that old cow," she said, "and I'm just the one to do it. It'll be my pleasure."

Kendra watched helplessly as her Aunt Jewel took Eula-Mae Bunch by the arm and pulled her to one side. They began to argue as Jeremy and Ginger hurried to Kendra's side.

"Isn't she great?" Jeremy said, admiring Aunt Jewel.

Sarah nodded. "Yeah, she really is. I wish I had her nerve. Come on, Kendra. Let's go get something to drink and leave them to their little discussion. You probably need it, after all that."

"But Aunt Jewel . . ." she started.

"Can take care of herself," Sarah added. "It's about time somebody told that old woman off. I was just about to do it myself, but it looks like Jewel's got her under control."

"Maybe you're right," Kendra said, taking one last worried glance at the two women before followed Ginger and Jeremy to the back porch for refreshments.

Fifteen minutes later, Jewel huffed up onto the back porch.

Kendra turned to her with a question in her eyes.

28

Aunt Jewel grinned. "Don't worry, honey. I took care of her. I doubt if she'll ever bother us again—not for a long, long time."

"Aunt Jewel! What did you do?"

Jewel looked surprised. "Why, nothin' that didn't need doin'. I just gave her a big old piece of my mind. Told her things that should have been said a long time ago." Aunt Jewel smiled. "It was so much fun, too."

Kendra breathed a sigh of relief. Eula-Mae Bunch had come close to ruining the entire workshop. She was sure that they hadn't heard the last from the nasty woman, but for now they had peace and quiet and could continue without interruptions.

"Where is she?" Sarah asked.

"Gone," Jewel said. "I personally showed her to the gate myself."

Good riddance, Kendra thought.

The ladies helped themselves to tea and cookies from a table set up on the porch. Some lingered in the shade, while the rest of the group wandered through Jewel's pride and joy—a raised-bed garden patterned after early Texas-style cottage gardens. The beds were edged with native limestone rocks that Kendra had gathered from the nearby countryside, and spilled over with bright, sun-washed colors of bachelor's buttons, hollyhocks and nicotiana.

Another bed contained a sprawling herb

garden filled with rosemary, oregano, thyme, catnip, basil and marjoram. In another bed along the property line grew the dye plants that Jewel used to make the traditional dyes.

The cough of a lawnmower next door caught Kendra's attention. It cranked then finally sputtered to life with a smoke-filled, deafening roar. "Oh no! Not now!" She groaned, turning to the group and shouting for them to return to the back of the house. What a time for him to do his lawn! Kendra thought. Could anything else go wrong?

Kendra was sorry she'd thought that when Alma and Oma Martin rounded the corner of the house and started screaming. Kendra, Ginger and Jeremy pushed through the crowd and were brought up short by the sight of Mrs. Bunch's ample body, laying very still, face down in a pool of deep, dark, blue indigo, a large silver hammer laying beside her head.

The first thought that went through Kendra's mind was that Aunt Jewel's three-year old batch of indigo had been destroyed.

Her second thought was that her Aunt Jewel must have whacked Mrs. Bunch over the head. She screamed and with a sigh of relief, saw her Aunt Jewel coming around the other corner of the house. She was with Nora Rogers and a few stragglers from the garden club.

Jeremy ran up to her, took one look at Kendra and smirked. "Whoa. Looks like Maxwell's been here."

"What?" she said, staring at him.

"You know, Maxwell's silver hammer came down on her head!" he warbled.

"Oh, right," she said. "I don't think this is the time for a joke, Jeremy."

"You're right, I'm sorry," he said, looking around. "You know me, I sing when I'm nervous."

Kendra reached down, avoiding the shards of broken glass. Trying not to disturb anything, she gently pressed her fingers to Mrs. Bunch's throat. She looked up into Ginger and Jewel's questioning eyes, then slowly shook her head.

"Ginger, call Sheriff Briggs for me, will you? And see if Jim's there while you're at it."

Ginger stood there for a second, staring down at Mrs. Bunch's body, then pulled her phone out of her jeans and stepped away from the crowd to call.

"Sarah, make sure nobody leaves," Kendra said. "I expect the sheriff will want to question everybody here." She nodded and left to gather the group together.

Kendra looked over at her Aunt Jewel, who had collapsed into a chair. Then she looked around for anything that seemed out of place. Everything was normal except for the body lying in the garden. Her neighbor's mower was quiet now, and the birds twittered in the trees like any normal day.

Except for the prone body, a bloody hammer and a deep, dark pool of indigo, there was no other indication that a woman had just been murdered in Aunt Jewel's garden amongst the blooming rosemary bush, the bright golden marigolds and the fragrant antique roses.

CHAPTER TWO

It only took Sheriff Buster Briggs and Deputy Jim Wyman seven minutes to drive to Jewel's house. The sheriff's office was conveniently located in the middle of downtown and adjacent to the Dairy Queen, which was also convenient for those mid-afternoon urges the sheriff often had for a butterscotch dip-cone with a Co-Cola chaser.

There weren't very many murders in Nameless, so this one got the sheriff's attention pronto. He pulled into the front driveway, sirens blaring and lights flashing. Deputy Jim Wyman pulled in behind him so fast he nearly rear-ended the sheriff's cruiser. After the dust settled a bit, the deputy jumped out of his car and marched up to the gate.

"Everyone stand back," he shouted then scurried over to the body before the sheriff had even turned off his car.

"Well, well—what have we got here?" he asked no one in particular. He nodded at Kendra, tipped his hat and looked down at Eula-Mae Bunch. He kneeled down beside the body and gingerly felt for her pulse. Shaking his head, he craned his neck around and peered at the crowd standing quietly to the side.

He sat back on his heels, pushed his hat back on his head and looked around him. "Looks like someone made one hell of a mess here."

The sheriff burst through the front gate, glaring at the crowd as if the women were in a line-up. Sheriff Buster Briggs was one of the tallest men Kendra had ever seen. He stood over seven feet tall, and he tended to fold himself in and out of cars, in and out of doorways. She often wondered how he managed to fit himself and his large hat into his cruiser.

"Don't nobody move, you hear?" he shouted, plowing through the group of women that hovered over the body. "Y'all get out of my way! This is an official investigation!"

"But Sheriff Briggs, you told us not to move," one of the women said. "Should we move, or should we get out of the way?" she asked.

The others nodded nervously and moved back a few feet.

He scowled at them, kneeled on the ground alongside Deputy Wyman, felt Mrs. Bunch's wrist for a pulse, then shook his head. "She's dead, Jim." He squinted up at Kendra through his dark glasses. "She's dead for sure. Would you like to tell me exactly what happened here, Miss Harper?"

"Ms. Harper, Sheriff Briggs," she corrected him and shrugged. "There isn't really much to tell. We are doing a workshop here for this group of ladies. We went out to the back porch to have refreshments and then came back around and found her."

"Is that so? It was as simple as that, was it? When you've been in this business as long as I have, you learn real quick that nothing is as simple as it looks from first appearances." He rose to his feet in slow motion, coiled like a rattler posed to strike.

Kendra fought hard to suppress a shudder. She never had liked snakes, and Sheriff Briggs reminded her of a big, fat, deadly one.

"Who exactly found this body?" he asked.

Kendra glanced around the crowd. Alma and Oma Martin stepped forward shyly. "We did, sheriff," Alma admitted.

"Uh huh. Y'all the ones with the goats, ain't you?"

"Sheep, sheriff. They're sheep, sir," Oma said.

"Sheep, goats, cows—farm animals are all the same to me. Six-of-one and half-a-dozen of the other. Would you two ladies like to tell me what happened here?"

"We were just walking back around the side of the house after having refreshments. We came around the corner and saw her lying there. That's all."

The sheriff looked down at the ground for a moment then turned his steely eyes to the two sisters. "Seems to me I remember some kind of a ruckus last year between you and the recently dearly departed here. You called me out to your farm. Am I correct?"

Oma nervously looked down at her shoes.

The sheriff crossed his arms over his chest. "Well, Miz Martin?"

The deputy walked over and smiled at Oma. "I remember what happened, sheriff. Some of the Martin's sheep got loose and ran through Mrs. Bunch's back yard."

"Oh, yes. It's all comin' back to me now. I seem to recollect that those sheep caused quite a bit of damage to her shrubbery. Is that right?"

"Yessir, it's true," Oma said, "but someone cut our fence. We couldn't help it if the sheep got loose. By the time we'd noticed it, several of them were out."

Alma spoke up. "If you remember, sheriff, Mrs. Bunch's son actually shot and killed one of our prize ewes. Then she tried to press charges against us."

The sheriff had already lost interest in the Martin's story. He slithered over to Aunt Jewel and nodded. "Miz Moore. Now why don't you tell me your version of this story?"

"Well, I . . ."

Sarah walked up and put her hand on Jewel's arm. "You don't have to say anything, Jewel, dear. The sheriff here hasn't read you your rights yet, after all."

"Should I?" the sheriff asked with a smirk.

"Besides, what do you know about it?"

Sarah backed off, shrugging. "Just trying to be supportive."

"Well," Verna Holt chimed in, "since Mrs. Moore here was the last one to see poor Mrs. Bunch alive, I assumed you would eventually get around to asking her some questions."

Kendra stared at the pastor's wife, not believing what she was suggesting.

Sarah frowned. "I would assume he'll ask ALL of us about what happened."

"Now look here, Mrs. Holt, the sheriff's not arrestin' anyone," Deputy Wyman drawled. "Yet."

"You can't believe that my aunt had anything to do with this, do you, Mrs. Holt?" Kendra asked.

"Well, dear. You know as the pastor's wife and a good God-fearing woman, I'm bound to tell the truth. I did see your Aunt Jewel arguing with Mrs. Bunch several times this morning."

"But I didn't kill her, for cryin' out loud!" Jewel blurted. "You should know that."

"Although," Mrs. Holt added, "I must say I didn't actually see her kill the poor woman."

A frown crossed Deputy Wyman's face and he glanced over at Kendra, raising his eyebrows.

"Why, this is ridiculous," Kendra said. "All of you know my Aunt Jewel would never hurt anyone. Admittedly, she didn't like Mrs. Bunch much. No one in town did. But she certainly didn't kill her."

"Hmph," the sheriff snorted. "We'll see about that. Deputy, gather up that hammer there and be careful with it. If it's got any prints on it, I don't want 'em all messed up."

"Yessir," he answered, scurrying off to get an evidence bag from his car.

The sheriff glanced over the crowd. His eyes came to rest on Ginger and Sarah, who stood to both sides of Kendra. "You two. You look like you're about to bust. What do y'all know about this brou-ha-ha?"

They look at each other, then nervously glanced at the ground.

Aunt Jewel stepped forward and looked up into the sheriff's dark glasses. "There's no need to bother these girls now, Buster. I can tell you exactly what happened. Eula-Mae was making a regular jackass out of herself, so I decided to give her a big piece of my mind. While the others were back on the porch having tea, I escorted her to the front gate and told her to get out and go on home."

"And then what happened?" he asked.

Jewel shrugged. "I'll admit we did argue a bit, but mostly because she couldn't believe that I was throwin' her out. I certainly didn't kill her. The last time I saw her, she was walking out the gate. She was mad as a wet hen, but she was alive."

"Did you actually see her drive away?" he asked.

"Well, no. I didn't," Jewel admitted.

38

"Officer! Young man! Sheriff, may I have a word with you?" A high-pitched voice called from beyond the fence.

"Oh no," Kendra groaned. "Just what we need—for him to stick his nose in this!" Kendra stared at their next door neighbor. Jack Adams was the nosiest and bossiest man that she had ever met. And she'd met a few. She called him (behind his back, of course) Jack-of-all-Asses because of his propensity to have an opinion on all subjects known to man. And to try to foist his opinions off on Aunt Jewel. He had retired way too early and had too much spare time on his hands that he spent minding the neighbor's business. Lots of time.

"And who are you?" the sheriff asked.

"Jack. Jack Adams. I live right next door." He pointed to a small, plainly painted white house with square shrubberies lining the walkway in military precision. He opened the gate and walked right through, almost stepping on Mrs. Bunch's body in the process.

"Oh dear. What a terrible mess. I was afraid something like this would happen. The goings-on over here you'd never believe."

Kendra stepped in front of him to stop his advance toward the sheriff. "Mr. Adams, please stay out of this. This is no concern of yours."

"That's never stopped him before," Jeremy said to Ginger in a low voice.

"Oh, but Ms. Harper, it most certainly *is* my concern."

39

"And why is that, Mr. Adams?" the sheriff asked.

He pointed to Jewel. "Because I saw her pick up that hammer and bash Eula-Mae Bunch over the head with it."

CHAPTER THREE

"You what?" Jewel gasped, her eyes flashing with anger.

Jack Adams retreated a few steps, and glanced around nervously. "That's right. I heard you out there arguing with Mrs. Bunch. I just happened to be looking in this direction, and I saw you pick up that hammer and bash that poor woman over the head with it."

"That's crazy!" she yelled. "I might have argued with her but I never bashed her over the head with anything."

"As much as she deserved it," Jeremy whispered to Ginger.

The pastor's wife stepped forward. "Sheriff. Deputy Wyman. If I may, I have something else to say."

The sheriff sighed. "Go on. I'm waiting," he said, crossing his arms over his chest.

"I've known Mrs. Moore here for ages, and I know for a fact that she wouldn't hurt a fly. She may have argued with Mrs. Bunch, but she surely didn't kill her. I'm almost positive of it."

"Are you callin' me a liar?" Mr. Adams shrieked. "I know what I saw! Who do you think you are, anyway?"

Verna swung around to face him. "I am *the* wife of *the* pastor, Garvey Holt, of the First Christian Baptist Free -Will church. And there's no need to shriek."

"Maybe you wouldn't mind tellin' us exactly that you think you saw once again. This time we'll go down to the office," Jim said. He faced the silent crowd of women standing to the side. "I'd like to talk to you ladies, too, if you don't mind."

"Aren't you going to arrest her, Sheriff ?" the neighbor demanded.

The sheriff shook his head. "Can't. Don't have one lick of evidence proving that she did or didn't kill Miz Bunch here. But don't you worry, Mr. Adams. We'll get to the bottom of this one way or another, pronto. And, Miz Moore, don't plan on leavin' town anytime soon." He looked at Kendra. "You neither."

Kendra gritted her teeth and watched the sheriff as he walked back out to his cruiser. "He just had to say that, didn't he?"

Jeremy smirked. "Of course. It's what all the cops on TV say, ain't it? I'll bet he watches a lot of TV cop shows."

Kendra had already had three cups of coffee at home and still couldn't get her eyes open the next morning. She decided to go into town to Do-

Lolly's Diner and have some of their "Guaranteed to Peel Your Eyelids or Your Money Back Pronto" coffee. She didn't think they'd ever had to give anybody's money back. She walked in and picked an empty booth in the back corner of the dining room.

"Jeepers, peepers, where'd you get them creepers?" a voice trilled from behind a menu, garbling the old song on purpose.

"Oh, hey there, Jeremy," she called to the blonde waiter who was slinking down the aisle, looking this way and that way before plopping down on the red vinyl seat across from Kendra. He wore the uniform of a Star Fleet officer and sported large, pointy pink ears made of rubber.

"Hey yourself, toots. How ya doin' today? The town's all-a-buzz about the hoo-hah over at your place yesterday."

"That figures."

"How's Aunt Jewel?" he asked.

"She's fine, I'm fine, and we're all fine. Don't I look it?"

"Weelll . . .You do look a might peaked." He reached over and tweaked her cheeks.

"All right already!" Kendra said, swatting his hands away from her face. "You know me too well for someone who isn't even kin to me."

"Frightening, isn't it?" he asked, grinning and scratching his right ear.

She stared at him for a moment. "Yeah, pretty

scary. Anyway, I'm OK, I guess. I was up half the night, though, worrying about Aunt Jewel and how we're gonna get her out of this mess."

"Nasty bit of business, wot?" He tapped his finger against his lips then lowered his voice. "You know, I believe there's a reward here in town for the first person to knock off Mrs. Bunch. If your aunt really did do it, then we'll be rich!"

"Jeremy! Don't joke like that! You know good and well she didn't do it. Besides, do you think we'd share the money with you?" she teased.

"Yeah, I know. But the truth is that someone did, and I'm not too sad about it, either. I'm not surprised at all that someone ended up killing that old Mrs. Bunch-of-Crap. Why, that woman's face is in the dictionary under the word *bitch*. She's nothing but a troublemaker. No one in town has a kind word to say about her. Her hobby was making trouble. She even tried to make trouble for Sarah, and you know how nice Sarah is to everybody."

"Sarah? What did she do to her?"

"Mrs. Bunch complained to the City Council about Sarah's sidewalk displays. Said they 'ruined the continuity' of the downtown design or some bullshit like that. She argued that it was a fire hazard."

Kendra frowned. "That is odd. Sarah didn't mention anything to me about Mrs. Bunch trying to make trouble for her. I thought they were friends. Sort of."

44

Jeremy continued. "And not only that, Mrs. Bunch even said that Sarah's displays were downright tacky."

The bell over the front door tinkled and Jeremy and Kendra turned to see Jewel enter and look around for an empty booth. Jeremy rushed to greet her, pulling her into his arms and kissing her soundly on both her cheeks. "Jewel, darling! Yesterday was simply ghastly! Do come in and have some café au lait and tell me all about it! I assume you do want to sit with your lovely niece?"

She sighed and glanced over at Kendra. "I suppose so."

He seated her at Kendra's booth and rushed to get another cup of coffee.

"How are you really doing today?" Kendra asked her. "You were still asleep when I left this morning."

Jewel snorted. "I wasn't asleep. I didn't sleep all night. I guess I'm about as well as can be expected, considering how lucky I am that I didn't end up spending last night in jail."

When Jeremy returned, he served coffee to Kendra and Jewel and poured a cup for himself. "Now!" he exclaimed. "Down to business," and crowded into the seat, pushing Kendra over to the window.

The owner of the diner, Lolly LaRue, came rushing over. "Jewel, I heard about what happened. I heard you really let her have it! Verbally, I mean.

It's about time someone told that old witch off. Pity you didn't really get a chance to kill her!"

"Lolly . . ."

"Yeah, yeah, I know. No killing allowed during the dyeing workshops. Get it—dyeing? Dying?"

Kendra gave her a look that would sear the paint off the side of a barn, but she chose to ignore it.

"Could I get an order of whole wheat toast, please?" Kendra asked. "If you're not too busy, that is."

Lolly waved her off and turned to Jewel. "Ok, ok! Never mind the jokes. So spill the beans—give me all the details."

"Sounds like you've already heard all about it. Why don't you tell us what happened?" Aunt Jewel replied with a grimace."I expect tongues are wagging in town."

"Actually, I do get the facts. All the facts, ma'am. You know that small town network is alive and kickin' here in Nameless! Somebody's got to spread the rumors and keep up with the innuendos," Lolly said.

"That's usually MY job," Jeremy sniffed.

Lolly ignored him and continued. "It must have been horrible for y'all! What with all the police tramping through your garden, and the bodies in your flower beds and all that blood to clean up!" She shuddered.

"Body. Just one body, Lolly," Kendra corrected her, then shrugged. "And there wasn't much blood to clean up, to speak of."

Jewel nodded. "But it did make a mess for sure. All that blue indigo. All over the place. We'll never get it all out of the bricks. I suppose we'll have to replace some of them now, Kendra," she sighed. "At least the stuff's organic."

"Well, nevertheless, I know exactly what you need," Jeremy said to Kendra.

"And what's that, Jeremy?" she asked, warily. "How about some toast?"

"You mean besides a man?" Aunt Jewel quipped, and the two of them smiled and high-fived.

Kendra frowned. "Very funny, Auntie. This is no time for you to start in on my state of singlehood. This is serious business. Sheriff Briggs thinks you whacked Mrs. Bunch over the head with a silver hammer and a jar full of indigo, and all you can do is sit here joking."

Aunt Jewel fought to compose herself. She reached over and patted Kendra's hand. "You're right, dear. I'm just trying to be optimistic. After all, we all know that I didn't really kill her. We need to figure out who did, though, so I won't spend the rest of my golden years crocheting doilies in the hoosegow."

"Whose what?" Jeremy asked.

Kendra rolled her eyes. "Never mind! That's

not going to happen. We'll figure out something. And in spite of the sheriff's suspicions, they have no evidence or proof that you killed her . . .except that Mr. Jack-of-all-Asses said he saw you do it."

Jewel cringed. "That man drives me nuts. He just wants us to move away so he can get our house. He's wanted it ever since we fixed it up and moved in. I don't know what he *thought* he saw, but he certainly didn't see me bash her over the head. I know we don't get along really well with him, but why take it out on me? Why would he lie like that?"

"Which brings me back to my earlier comment," Jeremy announced. "Kendra, you need someone to help you investigate this thing and find out who really killed Mrs. Bunch, so you can get your auntie here off the hook." He jumped out of the booth and flung his arms over his head. "I, Avid Avenger, am just that person!"

Jewel laughed. "Looks more like Big-Eared Avenger to me."

"Oh no, you don't," Kendra groaned. "Leave the crime detecting to the sheriff and the deputy."

"No offense, but Buster Briggs and Deputy Jim couldn't find their butts if they used both hands and a flashlight," smirked Jeremy.

"Now you leave Jim out of this," Kendra warned.

Jeremy looked at Aunt Jewel and they quirked their eyebrows.

He shrugged. "OK. So maybe your deputy could solve the case. But, you know that the sheriff is going to get in his way. What they both need is a little outside help."

"But Jeremy . . ."

"No, really, it'll be fun! The sheriff's so busy he can't see straight. I'm sure Jim would help you, but there's only so much he can do on his own without getting in trouble. I'll just keep snooping around—here a little, there a little."

"So what's new about that?" Aunt Jewel asked, taking a sip of her coffee.

Jeremy lifted his eyebrows and stared at the ceiling for a moment. "Like I was saying before I was so rudely interrupted, I'll snoop around here, and y'all can handle Part B of the plan. It's only logical."

"Part B?" Kendra asked.

"The plan?" her Aunt Jewel asked. "What plan?"

"Details . . .details. You ladies leave it to me. I hear all sorts of things in this diner that you would never believe."

Kendra took a look at his huge rubber ears. "I believe it."

He smirked. "Let me continue. The sheriff and Deputy Jim both come in here at least once a day, when they're not takin' their business over to the DQ. Almost everybody in town comes in here at least once a week. I can accidentally on purpose

49

overhear any conversation in this place. We can do this!"

Kendra shook her head and looked at Aunt Jewel.

Aunt Jewel shrugged. "What could it hurt, Columbo?"

Kendra knew that Jeremy was right about the sheriff. He wouldn't be working too hard to find Mrs. Bunch's murderer. Especially since he thought he already had an eyewitness who saw her aunt kill her. Maybe they should do a little snooping around themselves. It couldn't hurt, could it?

After breakfast, Kendra and Aunt Jewel decided to walk down the street and stop in at Sarah's Needles & Threads. Kendra's friend had promised to call her when her monthly shipment of new yarns came in. Aunt Jewel's birthday was coming up, and Kendra decided to surprise her with some luscious cashmere yarns she'd drooled over last time they were in. Sarah specialized in natural fiber knitting yarns and other needlework supplies and Aunt Jewel called it her "crafty crack connection."

The air was already humid and muggy by 10:00 a.m. when they walked into the shop. A sign on the door warned them not to let the cat out. A huge ball of black and white fur peered out the front window at people passing by. Kendra tapped on the glass and the cat yawned, rose to stretch, turned around three times then fell back into its identical position of a few moments earlier.

"Worthless beast," Aunt Jewel complained as they walked into the store, but she smiled at the cat and chucked him under the chin nevertheless.

"Well, hello you two!" Sarah called, rushing to the front of the shop to greet them.

Sarah Wilson had owned the yarn shop for over five years and when Kendra moved to Nameless they had become fast friends.

The small shop was old, cramped, cozy and colorful, and it made Kendra feel good just to be there. Kendra loved fondling the fibers herself, although she didn't enjoy knitting or needlecrafts herself. The walls were covered with the bins of colorful natural fiber yarns—cottons, linens, wools and silks—that were Sarah's specialty. A revolving rack on the countertop displayed shiny handmade stoneware buttons, and a wicker basket on the floor held an array of books and magazines. Knitting needles and accessories hung behind the counter. Brightly colored knitted samples fluttered all over the room like flags, illustrating what could be done with specific yarns. A small sitting area was clustered in a back corner around a bookshelf crammed with well-used books.

"I see His Highness there is hard at work,"

Jewel said, nodding towards the cat.

Sarah grinned. "Yes ma'am—just like always. Cracker's my official greeter." She turned to Kendra. "I meant to give you a call, but it's been crazy here this morning. The shipment came in earlier, but I haven't had a chance to open it yet."

"What shipment?" Jewel asked, and Kendra shot a warning glance at Sarah.

"Oh, she ordered a few books on folklore for me," Kendra lied, giving Sarah a look.

"Oh, right. The books," she murmured. "I'll give you a call when I get them unpacked."

Kendra smiled. "That's a good idea."

"Y'all really know how to put on a workshop!" Sarah said. "That was some day yesterday," she shook her head. "I can't believe that jackass next door actually said he saw you hit her over the head! What could he be thinking?" She lowered her voice and looked around the shop. "You know, Jewel," she whispered, "if we'd known you wanted to get rid of old Mrs. Bunch that badly, we could have poisoned her tea or something less messy. We wouldn't have had to waste all that beautiful indigo."

Jewel laughed. "That's what I like about my daughter's friends. They're always willing to accommodate an old lady."

"You know," Jewel said, "we've been joking about it, but I wonder who really killed Mrs. Bunch. I know I didn't do it . . ."

52

"Me neither," said Kendra.

"Nor I," said Sarah. "So, who did?"

"It's kinda creepy thinking someone we know is a murderer."

Kendra nodded. "Jeremy says Mrs. Bunch had a lot of enemies in Nameless. Ever since she retired from teaching, she's been doing nothing but causing trouble and making a general nuisance out of herself. That reminds me," she said to Sarah, "Jeremy told us that Mrs. Bunch had it in for you, too."

"He told you that?"

"Yeah, just this morning. He said the woman was complaining about your sidewalk displays."

Sarah shrugged. "Yeah, she did. It's no big deal. I didn't want to say anything about it because the whole thing was so incredibly stupid. She claimed that my displays were a fire hazard, and that they clogged up the flow of walk-by traffic on Main Street."

Jewel peered out the window and snorted. "What walk-by traffic on Main Street? Nobody comes down here just to browse—at least not hordes of people. And there's plenty of room to walk by. That woman had a screw loose somewhere."

"Yeah, that's what I thought," Sarah said. "I just decided to ignore her and hoped she'd give up sooner or later. She was going to take the matter before the city council at the next meeting, but now . . ."

"I don't understand what she had against you," Kendra commented.

"Apparently I wasn't the only one here on Main she had her crosshairs sighted on," Sarah admitted.

"Oh? Who else was she after?" Kendra asked.

"Nora Rogers."

"The librarian?" Jewel asked.

"Yep. Nora was in here the other day grumbling about how Mrs. Bunch had it in for her."

"Why?" Kendra asked. "She is one of the sweetest women I know. She's really done a lot with that library since she got hired two years ago. I can't fathom why anyone would have a grudge against her."

Sarah shook her head. "I don't know all the details, but apparently Mrs. Bunch didn't like the way Nora was handling things down there. Something about the book ordering system, I guess. That's all I know."

Kendra thought for a moment. "Aunt Jewel, why don't you stay here and visit with Sarah for a little longer? Maybe you can find a new knitting pattern book or something to keep your mind off of this ridiculous business. I'll be back in a little while and we can go home."

"And where are you going all of a sudden?" Sarah asked.

"To the library, of course," Kendra answered.

CHAPTER FOUR

The sun was baking the cement pavement as Kendra walked out of the coolness of Sarah's shop into the scorching midday sun. The temperature was close to 96-degrees which actually felt cool after the long stretch of over 100-degree days they'd had that summer. Of course, the month before the temperature had been 48-degrees. But that's Texas weather for you, Kendra thought. If you don't like it, wait a minute and it'll change. Or go around the block; the weather would be different there. It was always hotter downtown since there were no trees there to provide natural shade.

By the time Kendra had walked the two blocks down Main to the library, her hair was standing out from her head in damp curls. She welcomed the quiet and the coolness of the library, and hesitated for a few moments after entering to let her eyes readjust to the darkness inside the building.

An older man, almost skeletal in appearance, sat near the front windows reading a copy of the *Austin American-Statesman*. He nodded to her as she entered, smiled, and went back to his paper. Kendra felt that she should know his name. After all, Nameless was a very small town. She had been living here for almost three years now since running away from the frantic pace of life in Austin and moving in with her Aunt Jewel. It was very rare to walk into any establishment in Nameless and not run into somebody she knew, or somebody kin to somebody she knew.

Kendra walked over to browse the New Books section. She always looked here first to see if there were any new folklore books or ghost story collections. She was surprised to see that there were two new ones on cooking with herbs and saving seeds. She picked those up for Aunt Jewel, took them to the check-out desk and patiently waited in line behind a woman applying for a library card.

Nora Rogers was working behind the desk, and Kendra watched her as she helped the woman with her application. Kendra knew that Nora was near her age, around 35-years-old, but she already looked closer to 45. She was thin and had mousy blonde hair that she wore in a slightly out-of-date bouffant style, with lots of hairspray holding it in place. She looked tired, and her eyes were dark and smudged underneath. That wasn't a surprise, since Nora was a single mother with two kids to support. She was attending the University of Texas in Austin part-time, working on her Master's of Library Science degree.

Nora looked up as the woman left, and smiled at Kendra. "Hi there. Great workshop yesterday." She grimaced. "At least the first part of it."

Kendra rolled her eyes. "Yeah. Thanks. We had no idea that it would be quite so exciting and eventful."

Nora laughed. "I'll bet you didn't. How's your aunt holding up? Is she OK?"

"Yeah, I suppose. She hasn't talked much about it, really. What annoys her most is that Mr. Adams says she did it."

"Yes, that man is very annoying. Do you think he actually saw the murderer, though?" Nora asked quietly.

Kendra shrugged. "I don't know what he saw. That's what he says, anyway. That man's blind as a bat, or he was hallucinating. One thing for sure is that he did not see Aunt Jewel kill Eula-Mae Bunch."

Nora nodded. "Between you and me, he does have a reputation for drinking a bit. He's come in here a few times, drunk as a skunk and I've had to throw him out. Shoot, of course Jewel didn't do it! No one around here believes she did. It's kind of scary, though—don't you think? We were there all morning with a killer and didn't even know it."

"Yeah, I know," Kendra said. "But I don't really think the rest of us were ever in any danger. We were all behind the house when it happened. Somebody could have walked up off the street and

57

killed her." Although highly unlikely, Kendra thought.

Nora nodded. "That's right. Whoever killed Mrs. Bunch probably just finally got fed up with her and couldn't stand it anymore. She could be a real pain in the neck."

Kendra thought for a moment. "Nora, Sarah said Mrs. Bunch was trying to make trouble for you, too. Is that true?"

Nora hesitated. "I'm not sure. I know that for some reason she wasn't totally happy with my work here, but I don't know all the details. All I know is that she had a meeting scheduled with the Library Committee on the day she died. She called all the members and demanded that they meet with her. Obviously, she never made it to the meeting."

"Did you go to the meeting?" Kendra asked.

"No. I wasn't invited, and besides, the other members cancelled it when they heard what happened."

"Don't you think it strange that you weren't invited?" Kendra asked. "After all, you are the head librarian."

Nora smiled. "I'm the ONLY librarian. I'm not sure it was so strange. She was always trying to call special meetings like this. They made her feel important, I suppose. Mostly they're a waste of everyone's time. I certainly wasn't offended when I found out I wasn't invited. In fact, I was kind of glad."

"Do you have any idea why she called this special meeting?" Kendra asked.

Nora shook her head. "Not really. All I know is that she wanted to talk about our policy of book donations. It didn't sound very serious to me—certainly not serious enough to call a special meeting. But that was typical of her."

"Hmm. Well, I'd better get back over to Sarah's and pick up Aunt Jewel. She'll really like these books. Maybe they'll keep her mind off her worries for a bit."

"Tell her I said 'hi'. I hope you find the person who killed that woman so Jewel can rest easy." She looked around and lowered her voice. "I just might thank them personally. And Kendra, anytime you want to do a workshop here on folklore, I mean a full-day thing instead of just a short talk, just let me know. You could even do a display and hang some of your photos. But promise me, no dead bodies."

Kendra laughed. "OK—thanks! I just might do that. After I get Aunt Jewel cleared of this murder."

Nora frowned. "You're not playing detective, are you? That could be dangerous."

"Not really, but if Aunt Jewel does get arrested, I'd like to have something for the sheriff to go on besides Mr. Adam's story."

Nora nodded. "That makes sense. Good luck. And enjoy those new books."

"We will," Kendra said as she turned to leave, already thinking of her next move.

Kendra pulled her truck into the driveway and the two women climbed down out of the cab. Jewel started to walk through the back gate into the courtyard, then stopped, staring at the low rock wall next to Mr. Adams' yard. "Oh no," she said, her face turning white. She looked over at Kendra.

"What's wrong? You look like you've seen a ghost. What's the matter with . . ." Kendra stopped. And stared. Someone had practically decimated Aunt Jewel's prized indigo bush. The shiny dark leaves lay scattered around on the ground underneath a short, whacked-off stump.

CHAPTER FIVE

Whack!

"Maybe I should just run over him in the truck."

Whack!

"Kendra, you know you can't do that—you just got that truck," Sarah reminded her.

Whack!

"How about poison?"

"No, I don't think so," Jewel said. "That's too good for him. Besides, we don't need the sheriff snooping around here any more than he already is."

Whack!

"Maybe we could do something simple. Like tie him up, chop off his head, and put him in the compost pile," Ginger suggested.

"Umm . . . tempting, but a bit too messy. And he'd collect flies."

Whack!

"Hey, wait!" Sarah said. "What I think you should do is gather up all those lovely dandelion seeds we propagate so well in the back yard and accidentally on purpose let them drift next door onto his nice lawn."

Startled, they high-fived each other. "Yes! Perfect!"

Now that that weighty decision was made for the day, Kendra commenced chopping garlic and basil for pasta with pesto that they'd have later for dinner. Cooking was her therapy, and smashing a dozen cloves of garlic was helping her to work off some of her anger. She used the flat side of a meat tenderizer on each clove. It was much more effective than any other method she'd ever tried. The scent from the garlic and the fat leaves of the Sweet Basil from the garden was so strong it made her head swim.

"I still can't understand why he felt the need to cut the bush down," she said, shaking her head.

Kendra stood at the small kitchen island, staring out the dining room window at the garden, pondering the fate of her next-door neighbor. The one with the disgustingly noisy lawnmower. The one who hated her because he thought her old-fashioned garden was trashy. The one who measured the grass in his front yard with a small ruler he kept in his back pocket for such occasions. The one who had accused her aunt of murder. The one who had just decimated their prized indigo bush. The bush Aunt Jewel had lovingly and tenderly cultivated from a wee sprig three years before.

Whack! She gave the garlic one last smack, picked the skins out and scooped it all into the food processor, turning it on until the basil was thoroughly macerated. She poured in virgin organic olive oil and mixed until the leaves were a smooth paste.

"That smells SO good," Ginger said, looking up at Kendra. She sat at the scrubbed pine dining room table, sewing impossibly tiny beads onto a scrap of organza in an intricate design. Kendra knew that eventually it would become one of her wall creations. Ginger's long, red silky hair fell down in a cascade around her face. Kendra thought she looked like Cher, or maybe Cousin It, and wondered how she managed to keep from sewing her hair to the fabric.

Sitting next to Ginger in one of Kendra's straight-backed kitchen chairs was Sarah Wilson. She was using a hand-held drop spindle and was spinning some incredibly thin mohair yarn using a fleece she had bought at the county Fiber Festival the past spring.

Burrowed down at one end of the sofa was Aunt Jewel. She was knitting a heavy green wool sweater for Kendra that she might be able to wear for about a week next winter. Maybe. If they ever had a real winter. Jewel wore a faded tee-shirt that proclaimed "Ewe's not fat—ewe's fluffy." Every so often she cursed and threw the sweater to the floor. After a few minutes, she'd pick it back up and try again.

Virginia Marshall, Ginger's 14-year-old

daughter, sat next to Kendra's aunt. She was slaving over a needlepoint Christmas stocking that she had been working on for about a year. Kendra wondered how old she would be when she finally finished it.

As Kendra glanced around the room, she marveled how a diverse group of women had come together and stayed together for going on three years now, in spite of their busy personal and professional schedules. They met at Kendra's house because she often liked to cook on the weekends, giving Aunt Jewel a break. They often got samples of the food while they were there, reaping the benefits of her efforts. In fact, none of them had ever missed a meeting. They were bound together with a common thread, so to speak—the simple love for yarns, fabrics, threads, beads, buttons, and all the great stuff you could make from them. Kendra's interest was more appreciative than as a practitioner.

Tonight, she was the resident cook. They all loved to eat Jewel's and Kendra's kitchen creations. Even in the small town of Nameless, Texas, they had found each other and stuck together through all sorts of diversities—births, divorces, marriages, decimated indigo bushes—and murder accusations. Jeremy sometimes popped in when he wasn't busy with the theatre or working at Do-Lolly's.

Kendra seethed with anger for a moment, thinking about her neighbor, then tried to put the indigo incident out of her mind. She'd deal with that no-good, weed-whacking maniac later.

Virginia looked at Aunt Jewel with admiration. "I can't really believe that they'd think you could kill someone. That's pretty cool. I wish I'd been here."

"No you don't!" Ginger said. "It wasn't a pleasant experience. The last part of it, I mean. The workshop part was great!" she added.

"It was pretty funny though—seeing all those little old ladies tottering around in their heels and their hats and gloves—with smocks and aprons over their clothes!" Sarah said, laughing.

"Y'all ready for lunch?" Kendra asked, trying to change the subject. She was answered with a chorus of "just let me get these last three beads on," and "just let me finish this row," and "just let me spin up the rest of this little wad of wool."

Jewel brought out a cut-glass relish plate that had been her grandmother's and loaded it with green onions, juicy green olives, homemade pickles and cherry tomatoes. All but the olives were from her garden. Finally, all five of the women were happily munching chicken salad sandwiches and coleslaw and sipping tall, sweaty glasses of minty sweet iced tea on the covered back porch. They sat, eating quietly, enjoying the food and the company and admiring the garden.

Kendra tried not to look at the skinny stump that was the remainder of the indigo bush. As she

65

ate, she watched fat honeybees bounce among the blooming purple basil plants. Her two cats, Boo, a large, sleek, solid black male, and Spike, a small, runty orange female, rolled in the catnip, kicking up wood chip mulch and nipping at each other's tails.

What a perfect day, Kendra thought.

A car drove up and parked, then a voice called from the side yard, cutting into Kendra's peaceful musings. "Anybody home? Y'all back there?"

Deputy Jim Wyman sauntered through the wrought iron gate, nervously twirling his grey Stetson in his hands. "Afternoon, ladies." He nodded to them.

"Deputy, come on in," Jewel called.

"Howdy, Mrs. Moore."

She nodded. "Good to see ya."

"Hello, Kendra," he said, a faint blush coloring his cheeks.

"Hello, Jim."

He walked up to the porch, his eyes never leaving Kendra's. He stumbled over a watering can and almost fell head first into the rosemary bush.

The women smirked and glanced slyly at each other. "Barney Fife lives," Aunt Jewel murmured. The women giggled and Kendra turned to them with a frown.

"Y'all hush!" she hissed.

"What was that, Mrs. Moore?" the deputy

asked, brushing the dirt off his jeans.

"Oh, nothing, Jim," Aunt Jewel answered. "What are you doin' out this way in the middle of a work day? Come on up on the porch and sit down in the shade. Have some iced tea. And there's plenty of chicken salad, if you're hungry. Oh, wait . . . you're not here to arrest me, are you? Because that would just ruin my day for sure."

He grinned. "Nope. I'm not here to arrest you. Are you trying to bribe me with food? Cause that just might work."

Kendra smiled. "Then why are you here? You usually avoid our gatherings like the plague."

He grinned. "Yeah, I do. And for good reason. A fellow could get major damage done to his ego sittin' here with this group."

"Now Jim," Ginger said, "that's not true. Go inside and get that extra pair of knitting needles and grab a chair and we'll teach you how to knit."

He shuddered visibly with 'Real men don't knit' written all over his face. "No thanks. I just came by to give y'all an update on the Bunch case."

"Does Sheriff Briggs know you're here?" Aunt Jewel asked.

"No ma'am, he doesn't," he admitted.

"Aren't you afraid you'll be givin' me an unfair advantage—supposedly bein' the killer and all?" she teased.

He shook his head. "No ma'am. I know you didn't kill that woman. Shoot, you couldn't hurt a fly. But you know—with the sheriff—that's a horse of a different color. He finds it hard to ignore eye-witnesses. But be sure he's going to question Mr. Adams to make sure."

"*Alleged* eye witnesses," Ginger put in.

"Right. Anyway, here's the facts. Mrs. Bunch died of a blow to the head. We're not really sure which one killed her—that jar bein' smashed over her head, the hammer blows, or the fact that she hit her head pretty hard on the corner of the rock planter when she fell."

"Man, I always miss the good stuff!" Virginia blurted.

"Virginia, hush!" Ginger hissed.

She shrugged and looked down at her plate.

Kendra winced. "Does it matter which one of those things really killed her?"

Deputy Wyman shook his head. "It could, but probably not. The result was the same."

"Were there any fingerprints on the glass?" Sarah asked. "How about on the hammer?"

"Nope. Not a one. There was something else, though." He took a small notebook from his shirt pocket. "This is why I'm here. This list of books was on a scrap of paper she had in her jacket pocket. Seems kinda strange to me, and it might not mean anything, but I thought I'd run it by y'all and see what you thought."

68

Ginger took the list and read over it. Frowning, she handed it to Kendra.

"Hmm, curiouser and curiouser. *Origin of the Species* by Charles Darwin, *Love's Wild Embrace* by Adora Lake, *Lady Chatterley's Lover* by D. H. Lawrence and *I Know Why the Caged Bird Sings* by Maya Angelou," she read out loud.

"Maybe it was a shopping list," Virginia said, grinning.

"Right!" Jewel hooted. "I can just see Mrs. Bunch reading a book called *Love's Wild Embrace*, much less the others."

"This is odd. It might not mean anything, but most of these are books that have been banned, or somewhat controversial in some way." Kendra frowned. "I'm not familiar with this one by Lake, though. Sounds like a romance novel to me."

Jewel nodded. "It *is* a romance. It's supposed to be pretty good. I've heard that it was written by a local author."

"From Nameless?" Ginger asked. "Seriously?"

Jewel nodded. "Yep. But no one really knows who she is."

Kendra looked at her aunt suspiciously. "How did you find that out?"

She shrugged and smiled. "I have my sources."

Ginger, Kendra, Jim, Virginia and Sarah looked at each other. "Jeremy," they said simultaneously.

69

Jewel smiled mysteriously. "Maybe, maybe not. Anyway, whoever wrote it is tryin' to keep it a secret, cause it's a bit—how shall we say—torrid—for Nameless. At least that's what I heard."

"Uh huh," Kendra said. "I see."

"Kendra, I thought I'd go next door and talk to Mr. Adams for a minute," Jim said. "Would you like to come with me?"

Kendra pondered for a moment. "Yes, I would. I'm still so mad I can't see straight. If I go over there by myself, no telling what I'll say. But if you go with me . . ."

"I can protect him," he said.

"Very funny, Deputy," she answered. "I'll be back in a bit. Y'all save me some tea."

Kendra and Jim walked along the street, carefully avoiding Mr. Adam's pristine grass. All of that flat lawn made Kendra's skin crawl.

The deputy knocked on the door and within a few seconds Mr. Adams answered. He hesitated, then motioned for them to come in, but didn't ask them to sit down.

Kendra hadn't been in Jack Adams' house since his wife died a few years back. She was struck speechless. Every possible inch of the room was filled with what she could only describe as junk—china knick-knacks lined the end tables and the coffee table. A large collection of salt and pepper shakers was collecting dust on the windowsills and shelves. Old newspapers and paperback books teetered in stacks in the corners and beside the old, threadbare sofa. An old black and white television sat in one corner, the picture flickering with the sound turned down.

"Deputy Wyman, what brings you over here?" he asked. "Sheriff Briggs has already asked me at least a thousand questions."

"I know. I just wanted to check a few things with you. First, though, we have another bit of business to take care of. Kendra told me they had a bit of damage to their property. Do you happen to know anything about Mrs. Moore's indigo bush that unfortunately has been destroyed?"

"Indigo? Shoot, Deputy, I don't know a pyracantha from a python. Why would I know anything about her indigo bush?" he smirked. "Probably kids—neighborhood vandals. Buncha hoodlums, you ask me. They probably did it."

Kendra suddenly found her tongue. "You whacked it down and now you deny it? You're blaming it on kids?"

The deputy shot Kendra a look that said he'd handle this. "Well, Mrs. Moore seems to think that you maybe . . . uh . . .trimmed a bit too close to the little rock wall out there and cut it down."

Mr. Adams shrugged. "I don't think so. Maybe she cut it down and is blaming it on me."

Kendra seethed, but tried to stay calm. She took a deep breath. "Look, Mr. Adams. That indigo bush was important to us. It took me three years of

71

tending it to get it that large, and you come along and whack it to the ground. I think you should make adequate compensation for it."

"I'll tell you what, Miss Harper. I'll go down to the nursery tomorrow and get you something prettier to replace it with. Something we can all appreciate. Now I'm not saying that I did cut it down, but I never did like the looks of that shrub anyway. Too spindly. Why don't I get you something that we can both enjoy? How about a nice nandina?"

Kendra thought that she had never been angrier in her life, until Adams opened his mouth again. "Say, deputy, when is the sheriff going to arrest her aunt for killing Mrs. Bunch? I don't see how he can loll around like he is, when he has a reliable eye-witness to the murder."

Kendra clenched her teeth and raised her hand to slap Mr. Adams right across the face, but Jim grabbed her arm and stopped her. She took a deep breath and squared her shoulders. "Mr. Adams, just exactly what is it that you think you saw my aunt do?"

"Kendra, let me handle this," Jim said gently.

"Go on Mr. Adams, you've told the sheriff what you saw, now tell us," Jim demanded.

"It's just like I told the sheriff. I was just about to mow my back yard, minding my own business . . ."

"Spying on us, is what he was doing," Kendra

commented.

"Minding my own business," Jack continued, "when I hear two women arguing real loud. I don't think anything about it, and continue to mow. I cut off my mower and pushed it around to the side, and that's when I saw them. They were still arguing, standing right over there in her yard. Except this time they were louder."

"And who were these two women?" Jim asked.

"One was Eula-Mae Bunch. She was facing out towards the street. And the other one was Mrs. Moore." He pointed to Kendra. "Her Aunt Jewel. Then, she reached back on the table there, picked up that jar with that green stuff in it, and bashed poor Mrs. Bunch over the head with it." He nodded. "That Bunch woman tottered around for a moment, then Jewel Moore picked up some kind of metal thing and whacked her with it. That's when she went down. That's what I saw."

"You lying son of a . . ." Kendra started.

"Kendra, be careful," Jim warned.

She turned around and slammed out of the front door, leaving him to deal with Mr. Adams.

As she stalked back home, she noticed a dark sedan parked across the street from the Adams' house. The driver ducked down in the seat as she passed, but she still got a glimpse of the blonde wig and the pointed ears. In spite of her anger, Kendra smiled. Jeremy was on the case.

CHAPTER SIX

"You know," Jeremy whispered, pulling at his collar, "churches are scary. It's so dark in here. I keep thinking that the creature from the Black Lagoon is gonna come up out of that pool of water up there. Or something squishy with long tentacles and suckers."

"Shh!" Aunt Jewel hissed, swatting at Jeremy as she looked for a place to sit. "That's the baptismal."

"The what?"

"The baptismal—where they baptize people."

"Oh," he said, raising his eyebrows and looking around the church. "How dismal, the baptismal."

Kendra shot him a warning look that said *don't mess with Aunt Jewel today*. Jeremy had begged Kendra to let him go to Mrs. Bunch's funeral with them, and they'd finally consented. They swung by the café to pick him up, and he reluctantly removed his rubber ears when Jewel refused to let him in the car. Otherwise, Kendra thought he looked fairly normal—whatever that was. It wasn't often that she saw him in clothes that weren't theatrical.

The organist was playing softly and the people were gathering one by one to pay their respects to Mrs. Eula-Mae Bunch. There were a large group of women from the Nameless Garden Club sitting close to the front, and Verna Holt was sitting on the front pew, staring at her husband. He sat quietly beside the pulpit, looking down at his shoes. Pastor Garvey Holt was tall, thin, and looked somewhat like an older Ken doll, Kendra thought. His skin was stretched tightly across his face, like a woman who's had one too many face-lifts. Kendra wondered if the pastor had had plastic surgery. He was dressed in a navy blue suit, with a bright red tie. A diamond tie-tack gleamed in the light.

Kendra glanced back at the door and noticed Sheriff Briggs come in, glance around, and finally take a seat close to the back. She nudged her aunt. "The sheriff's here," she whispered.

"That's because the murderer is probably here, too," Jewel whispered back.

"Really?" Jeremy squealed. "Cool."

"That wouldn't be hard," Kendra commented, ignoring Jeremy and glancing around the room. "It seems that everyone in town is here."

Deputy Wyman walked in the back door of the church, looked around, nodded at the sheriff and proceeded up the aisle to Kendra's pew. "Mornin', Mrs. Moore, Kendra. Hey Jeremy. Do y'all mind if I sit here?"

"Of course not, Jim," Jewel said, scooting over so he could have the seat beside Kendra. She frowned at her aunt, and then turned to the deputy.

"Hi there. I'm surprised to see you," she said.

The deputy glanced back at the sheriff. "Sheriff Briggs thought it might be a good idea for us to be here today."

Jeremy smirked. "Do y'all expect someone to jump up and run to the front yelling 'I did it! I killed her'?"

"Nope. We won't get that lucky. But you never know. Murderers often show up at the funerals of their victims."

Jewel raised her eyebrows and looked across at Kendra. An "I told you so" gleamed in her eyes.

Oma and Alma Martin came in and sat in the pew right behind them. They were followed by Nora Rogers, who entered and found a seat towards the front. Kendra thought it odd that the Martin sisters were there. She supposed they were as curious as anybody else.

She looked around one last time as the pastor rose to speak. It did look as if everyone in town had come to pay their last respects to a woman that seemed to be a friend to no one.

Pastor Holt nodded to the organist, and the music dwindled to an ear screeching halt.

"My friends," the pastor's voice boomed, "we are here to pay our last respects to Mrs. Eula-Mae Bunch, a pillar of this community and a very dear friend to many of us here."

"If he doesn't watch out," Jeremy whispered to Kendra, "his nose will start growing!"

"Shh!" Jewel hissed at him.

"Or he'll get struck by lightning," Kendra answered.

The pastor continued. "She was a good citizen of our town, and spent many hours with the Nameless Garden Club, helping to beautify our city. She also put incredible energy into working in our schools and our Public Library on various committees."

After a pause, he continued. "Although at times Mrs. Bunch could test our patience, it behooves us today to remember her for her good deeds." The pastor exchanged a quick glance with his wife, who looked down at her lap and started fidgeting with her purse and gloves. Today she wore a crisp cotton shirtwaist dress with a little navy bolero jacket over it. Her gloves matched her jacket and hat. Kendra wondered how many hats that woman owned. A sparkly brooch was pinned to her shoulder.

Aunt Jewel looked over at Kendra and raised an eyebrow. "Wonder what he meant by that remark?" she whispered.

Kendra shrugged, and turned her attention to the citizens of Nameless who were crowded into the little church. Nobody looked totally innocent, she thought.

Suddenly the back door of the church flew open, and a man Kendra didn't recognize stumbled into the room.

He was dressed in a rumpled gray suit and wore an outdated tie that hung unevenly. His dark hair was uncombed, and he had an uncanny resemblance to Mrs. Bunch. He glanced around wildly as if he was looking for someone in particular.

Pastor Holt stopped speaking in mid-sentence and blanched.

Mrs. Holt turned in her seat to see what her husband was staring at. Her face turned white as a ghost. She swayed in her seat as if she were about to faint, but then seemed to compose herself and she took a deep breath. She bowed her head and stared into her lap.

The man stumbled down the aisle. To the relief of Pastor Holt, he finally fell into an empty seat in the middle of the sanctuary near the center. Everyone reluctantly turned their attention back to the pastor, who took a deep breath and sat down suddenly, motioning for the choir to sing.

Jeremy whispered to Kendra. "I think that's Eula-Mae's son, but I'm not sure. Notice the resemblance."

She turned back to stare at him and nodded.

The navy-blue robed choir obviously was not ready to sing, but the pastor waved frantically at them and they rose shakily and belted out a

78

raucous rendition of *Amazing Grace*.

Aunt Jewel looked over at Kendra, a question in her eyes. She shrugged, and then turned to Jim.

"Is that her son?" she whispered.

"Shh!" Jeremy warned. "I love this song—although you couldn't dance to it if you tried."

Jim frowned at Jeremy and turned his attention back to Kendra. "Yes, that's him—Harry Bunch."

"Told ya so," Jeremy said.

"I didn't even know she had a son until recently. I've never seen him around here before."

"You probably wouldn't have," Jim said. "He pretty much keeps to himself. I met him for the first time last year when I had to go over there on account of Mrs. Bunch's dead roses and the Martin's dead sheep."

"So. He's the one who killed the Martin's prize ewe." She turned around slightly so she could see him. Harry Bunch was slumped in his seat and appeared to be asleep. Every once in a while he would look up, glance around and mumble something. Kendra wished she were sitting closer so she could hear what the man was saying. He appeared to be intoxicated, or drugged.

Apparently Jeremy read her mind, because all of a sudden he started coughing. Jewel quickly rummaged in her purse and handed him a cough drop, but he hissed at her, "Not now!" and got up out of his seat. He excused himself, choked out the word "Water!" between hacking coughs, and disappeared out the back door.

Aunt Jewel looked over at Kendra, but she just shrugged and innocently turned her attentions back to the choir. In another minute she heard the back door slowly and quietly open again, and out of the corner of her eye she saw Jeremy come back into the sanctuary and take a seat right beside Harry Bunch.

Smooth move, Jeremy, she thought. He seemed to have recovered nicely.

The man was oblivious to his surroundings and continued mumbling.

Much to the relief of the congregation, the choir finally finished their song and sat down.

Pastor Holt rushed through the rest of the service and motioned for the choir to sing once more. After they stumbled through another song, he mumbled the closing prayer and he and his wife quickly disappeared out the side door.

Jeremy looked around. "Is it over?"

As everyone rose to leave the church, Jewel shook her head. "That was the most bizarre funeral service I've ever seen in my life."

Kendra mumbled an agreement then turned to Jim with a tenuous smile.

"How about some lunch?" he asked. "I've got the rest of the day off, and I thought we could. . ."

"I'm sorry, Jim," she interrupted him. "I have a meeting with Nora at the library in about an hour.

80

We need to discuss a talk I'm doing there for them at Halloween and hash out some of the details. Before then, I have to take Aunt Jewel and Jeremy back home and go get my sketches and my camera."

"Your camera?"

"Yeah. I thought I'd take some photos of the church graveyard so I can have something to use to illustrate my talk. It'll make it spooky and inspire me. And you know how I love spooky."

He sighed, disappointed. "I get the picture."

"Sorry, honey," she said. "I'll tell you what. Aunt Jewel and I are going to Do-Lolly's later for dinner. Why don't you come by and join us?"

"OK, I guess," he admitted grumpily, then took her chin in his hand and smiled. "But I'd rather be alone with you. We've had so little time to ourselves lately."

Kendra smiled. "I know. We've both been working all the time, and now this thing with Aunt Jewel. I just can't give you my full attention now. Not like I want to."

The hangdog expression on his face melted her heart.

"Look. After dinner, you can come over and we'll do something fun for a change."

"Like?" he said, instantly perking up.

"Like maybe watching a movie? Or making popcorn?" Kendra said.

"Um . . .I'm listening."

"And sitting side by side on the sofa?"

"Um hmm . . .then what?"

"Then . . .you'll go home and I'll start making notes for my presentation," Kendra said.

"Ugh. Not work."

"Unless . . ."

"Unless what?" he whispered.

"Unless you can talk me out of it."

He grinned, tipped his hat, and drawled, "I'll surely try my best, ma'am, I surely will. I can be mighty persuasive when I have to be." He kissed her on the cheek and sauntered off to his car, whistling.

Kendra smiled and touched her cheek. "Don't I know it, deputy. Don't I know it."

Kendra met her aunt and Jeremy at the car. He ran to open her door for her. "Your chariot awaits, madame," he said with a bow and a sweeping motion of his arms.

"Please Jeremy," she laughed, "no bowing to me in the parking lot of the Baptist church."

"Oh. Right." He nodded towards Jim's car as it pulled out of the parking lot. "So. I saw you in deep communication with Deputy Dawg."

She frowned. "Hey!"

"Don't get huffy, I was just wondering if he said anything about our mystery man?"

"Not much," she said as she pulled out of the church driveway. "Apparently that *was* Mrs. Bunch's son, Harry, just as you suspected. He's the guy who shot the Martin's sheep."

"Ah," Aunt Jewel said. "I thought he looked familiar. There is a strong resemblance between those two. Or at least there was, before she—well, you know. Anyway, I haven't seen him around town for quite a while now." She shook her head. "He used to be so handsome and friendly. He looks kinda sickly now."

Jeremy snorted. "He looks pickled, you ask me," Jeremy said. "And smells it, too." He fanned his hand in front of his nose.

Kendra laughed. "By the way, that was some smooth move back there, Sherlock."

"What do you mean?" Aunt Jewel asked.

"Aunt Jewel! His coughing fit, of course!" She turned to Jeremy. "Pretty slick—so did you hear anything useful?" she asked him.

"You mean he was pretending? And to think I offered you a cough drop!" Jewel swatted him with her purse.

"Aunt Jewel! Please! So, Jeremy, spill the beans. What did he say?"

He shrugged. "Not much, unfortunately. It was all so garbled. I'm afraid my heroic efforts were entirely wasted." He shook his head. "It was just a bunch of gobbledygook."

"Rats! Are you sure? Try to remember what

he said exactly," she urged him.

He looked uncomfortable. "Well, I can't be certain, but . . .I think he said something about 'loving a cake.'"

"What?!"

"Loving a cake—that's what I said! I told you it didn't make sense."

Kendra shook her head and Aunt Jewel started laughing. "All of that hoo-hah for nothing! I can't believe you two!"

Kendra pulled up in front of her Aunt Jewel's house. "Out. Goodbye. See you later. So long."

Still laughing, Jewel climbed out of the car with a wave to Jeremy. "See you two secret agents later. Y'all try to stay out of trouble."

Kendra was silent as she pulled back onto the road and headed for Jeremy's apartment.

"Look, Kendra. I'm sorry. I didn't hear anything else. The guy was incoherent. He was mumbling. I couldn't get real close to him. The choir was singing, and . . ."

"Never mind, Jeremy," Kendra said wearily. "You did what you could."

"Besides, that guy might not even know anything about his mother's murder. I think he was just prostrate with grief and drunk as a skunk to boot. We've just started our investigation. We'll do better next time."

"We?"

"Well . . . I'll do better next time," he said, a

84

serious look on his face. "Look, Kendra. I certainly don't want to see Aunt Jewel go to jail any more than you do. I'll keep shaking the grapevine at the cafe and see if any monkeys fall out."

"All right," Kendra grinned in spite of herself. "And Jeremy . . ."

"Yes, doll face?"

"You're a pretty good sleuth, but you need to work on your surveillance techniques. I saw you last night skulking around my neighbor's house."

"You did? How did you know it was me? Gee, I borrowed my cousin's car and dressed in black and everything so I wouldn't be recognized."

"I knew it was you. It was pretty obvious."

His eyes narrowed. "Why?"

Kendra grinned. "You forgot to take off your Spock ears."

"Oh."

CHAPTER SEVEN

Kendra wiped the palms of her hands on her denim skirt and took a deep breath. She knew there was really no reason that she shouldn't take photos of the church graveyard, but figured Pastor Holt would want her to get permission first. She shrugged. Easier to get forgiveness than permission, Aunt Jewel always said. She planned on using the shots as background for her Halloween presentation. The small white clapboard church was built in the early 1800s, and the small cemetery behind the building had quite a few original tombstones in it. Kendra loved exploring the old cemeteries in the area, finding pioneer graves and historical markers.

She felt that if any real ghosts were in the area, they were bound to hang around places like the church cemetery.

It was almost dark when she arrived, but still light enough to take some shots. She could always lighten them up with Photoshop once she got home.

Kendra parked in back of the church in the area closest to the cemetery. She got out of her truck and walked around the corner of the church, towards the parking lot. A yellow Mercedes sat under the dim parking lot light beside an older blue Toyota Corolla. Kendra knew the Toyota was Nora's car.

Kendra heard loud voices in the sanctuary, so she ducked back behind the cars. As they got louder, she recognized Pastor Holt's voice, and then his wife's. She didn't know what they were arguing about, but it was a heated conversation.

She quickly took a few photos of the graves, deciding to come back during the daytime when she could read more of them.

She heard a loud noise, then a cry. The side door leading to the office hallway was open just a crack, and through the window Kendra could see the silhouettes of two figures. It didn't take long for her to realize that they were not arguing. They were in a close embrace, a rather hot clench, kissing. Passionately.

Kendra tried to decide what to do. She finally crept around to the front door and entered the building. She wrinkled her nose against the musty smell of the flowers from Mrs. Bunch's funeral. The cloying scent of carnations and lilies still permeated the air. Kendra sneezed, then walked through the quiet sanctuary. At that time of night, it was dark and spooky. The parking lot light shining through the stained glass windows was eerie and beautiful.

Kendra focused her camera and took several shots of the back wall, and was turning to photograph the opposite one when she again heard voices. She crept closer to the office hallway and listened.

At first she didn't understand what she was hearing. All she knew was that it certainly wasn't part of Pastor's Holt's sermon. The two voices sounded like they were reading from a play script—a very *steamy* script. Part of the dialogue made Kendra blush. She turned to leave, accidentally knocking over the vase on the piano.

"Who's there?" Pastor Garvey Holt shouted.

Kendra tried to duck down behind a pew, but wasn't fast enough. The Holts came running into the sanctuary and saw her standing there. They flicked on the lights and she squinted in the glare.

"What on earth are you doing?" Verna Holt demanded. "How long have you been here?"

"I just got here," Kendra lied. "The lights were so beautiful in here, through the windows, I mean. I thought I'd take some photos. I'm so sorry about the vase; I'll replace it. I'd like to just take a few photos of the cemetery if I can," she rambled. "I'm doing a presentation in October for the library. I wanted to take a few outside in the graveyard, if that's not a problem. The church is so old, and I thought . . ." She continued on, hoping that something would distract them from the fact that she was inside, in the dark. Listening to their performance.

Pastor Holt frowned. "Isn't it a bit dark for

taking pictures?" he asked.

Oops. Guess not.

Kendra smiled. "The better to see the ghosts in here."

He frowned and crossed his arms. "I don't really see the humor in that, young woman."

"I can always lighten the photos using software if I have to," Kendra said.

Mrs. Holt glanced at her husband. "We'd rather you didn't, but I suppose it's OK to take a few pictures."

"Do you mind if I take your photo?" Kendra asked.

"Why would you want to do that? Verna asked.

Kendra shrugged. "No special reason. I just need to practice with this new camera." She was at a loss for words, but said the first thing that came to her mind. Before Verna could reply, Kendra raised the camera, pressed the button and the camera whirred.

"I'd rather you didn't," Verna said.

Kendra shrugged. "OK, it doesn't look like the flash is working anyway. These are just for my own notes. Don't worry, they won't be published in the newspaper," she joked. "I always take photos of sites so I can look at them before I start to write."

Mrs. Holt frowned and Kendra was certain she glared at her for a few seconds. "I see. Well,

I'm not so sure . . ." the pastor's wife started.

"Well, I'll just be on my way now, take a few more photos outside..." Kendra said. She turned to leave, then turned her attentions back to Mrs. Holt. She was wearing a remarkably unwrinkled yellow linen suit with a navy jacket and gloves and carried a navy straw hat and purse. A large diamond and sapphire brooch was pinned to her left shoulder. It looked like an antique.

Kendra nodded towards the jewelry. "I noticed your brooch earlier. It's beautiful. Wherever did you find one like that? Is it vintage?"

Mrs. Holt's hand flew to her breast and then to the pin. "Yes. Ah . . . it's been in my family for ages. I inherited it from my grandmother when she passed on."

"I thought maybe you bought it at the antique store here in town," Kendra surmised.

"This? Oh no! Pastor could never afford something like this on his own—not on his salary!"

He smiled. "She's right about that."

"Well, it's certainly beautiful."

Mrs. Holt fingered the brooch. "Yes," she murmured, "it is, isn't it?" She laughed nervously. "Of course, I really shouldn't wear it at all. It's so extravagant—so showy. It's really a vain thing for me to do. You know what the good Lord said about storing our riches here on earth."

"Uh. Sure." No problem there for me, Kendra thought. "Look. I'd better go now. I'll just take a few more photos outside and be on my way. I can always come back later if I need more."

Just then, Nora Rogers walked in and halted when she saw Kendra. "Oh, I'm sorry. Am I interrupting? I think I left my scarf here this morning and wanted to see if I could find it since I was here anyway."

Mrs. Holt smirked. "I'm sure it's not here in the sanctuary. The custodian would have put it in the office if it was here when they cleaned earlier."

Nora smiled. "That's fine; I guess I'll check on Monday, then."

Kendra looked at Nora. "Would you mind waiting for me? I'd like to ask you a question about the presentation."

Nora frowned. "Sure, I'll meet you in the parking lot. I have a little bit of work I need to do here in the library."

At Kendra's puzzled look, she explained. "I'm trying to organize the church membership records for the historical archives at the public library."

Kendra nodded. "I'll be here for a while, no hurry," she said. "I want to take a few more outdoor shots tonight."

Pastor Holt shook his head. "It would be best if we all went home, I think. It's been a long day for all of us. And Kendra, in the future, it's better not to come poking around here at night."

Kendra quickly said her goodbyes and left the church. She took a few more photos in the graveyard, focusing on the oldest residents, then put her bag and camera in her truck.

Kendra trudged through the weeds at the edge of the dusty gravel path to the church and was wishing she'd worn something cooler. The night was still warm—hot, even. When she got back to the parking lot, Nora was calmly leaning against the blue Toyota with her face to the moon, eyes closed. Kendra called out and she opened her eyes.

"Hi. You caught me," she laughed nervously.

"Caught you?" Kendra asked.

"Yeah. I was actually resting for a minute." She nodded towards the church. "I really don't have time to do this."

"Do what?" Kendra asked.

"Oh, they're trying to talk me into joining the church library committee. What with my classes, and my kids, and the library job, I don't have time for one more thing. I just took a look at their system. It's a big mess. All the historical stuff is good for the public library; I don't mind doing that."

Kendra nodded towards the church. "So what was that all other stuff about? Did you hear it?"

"What do you mean?" Nora asked.

"I heard noises, and a lot of, uh, other stuff. It sounded like somebody was rehearsing a play or something." Kendra didn't mention that she'd seen two people—well, two silhouettes, anyway—in a romantic clench.

Nora shrugged. "Must have been before I came by. Maybe they're working on the Thanksgiving pageant?"

Kendra laughed. "No, I'm pretty sure it wasn't that."

Nora shrugged. "I don't have the foggiest idea, then."

"Listen, Nora, I know you're busy, but there's something I wanted to ask you," Kendra said.

"Ask away."

"Deputy Wyman said that they found a list of book titles in Mrs. Bunch's purse after she was killed." Kendra pulled the list out of her pocket. "Take a look at this and see if it means anything to you."

Nora took the list, held it up to the light and scanned it quickly. She shrugged. "It's a list of books that are controversial."

Kendra nodded. "Yeah. That's what I thought, too—books that have been banned from area schools. I read something about that in the newspaper recently."

"Right," Nora said, tapping the list. "All except for this one—*Love's Wild Embrace*. It's a pretty steamy romance. We just got it in at the library. I keep waiting for the complaints to flood in, but so far, no problems." She frowned. "Seems like I heard that the author lives around here."

"And you don't know who this Adora Lake person really is?"

Nora shook her head. "No, but I wish I did. I'm kinda curious myself."

"Have you read this book?"

Nora grinned. "Not yet, but I will when I get the time. It's supposed to be pretty good. We have a copy in the library and it's been checked out almost constantly since we got it in a few months ago."

"Don't you read all the books before you buy them?"

Nora shook her head. "I wish I had the time to do that. We rely mostly on reviews in the various library journals for our purchases. But that book wasn't purchased by us. It was donated to the library. It came in with a sack of old magazines for our exchange table, although it is a new copy. I don't even know who gave it to us."

Nora handed the list back to Kendra. "If I could guess, I'd bet that was the reason Eula-Mae wanted to call a special meeting of the Library Committee. She probably wanted to squawk about our book selections again."

"Again? So she's caused trouble for you before?"

Nora laughed. "You could say that. That woman has been nothing but trouble for me since I came to Nameless."

"Why?"

Nora hesitated then shrugged. "Who knows? I think she just likes to call all the shots. She wanted control over all library book purchases, and my stand on non-censorship conflicted with that."

"Um. Speaking of the library, I'd better get to work on my Halloween presentation."

"Oh, come on, you have a whole month before that's due."

Kendra grimaced. "Yikes, no pressure, right?"

Nora laughed. "None at all."

"It's my first local one, and I want to do it right." And hopefully, Kendra thought, it will lead to many more opportunities here in town.

Nora nodded. "Good girl. I'd better let you get to work, then. I'll see you later." Nora started to get into her car.

"Hey Nora?" Kendra yelled as she walked back towards her truck. "Next time *Love's Wild Embrace* comes into the library, reserve it for me, will you? I haven't been able to find it in any of the bookstores."

Nora grinned. "Sure. See ya later."

Kendra looked up to see the pastor's wife getting into the powder yellow Mercedes. Verna Holt suddenly looked pale and wilted in the heat. She had removed her jacket and gloves and had an iron grip on the steering wheel of the car. She looked disheveled, like she'd been tromping through a weed field.

95

As Kendra passed her on the way back to her own truck, she waved and smiled, but Verna didn't even notice. When Kendra got to her truck, she noticed that the door was ajar. She cautiously glanced around but the only people there were long dead, and of no danger to her. She shrugged and climbed up into the truck and drove home.

CHAPTER EIGHT

"So . . .who ordered the pig snouts with gravy?" Jeremy asked, slinging a plate of chicken fried steak in front of Kendra. He had changed back to the same old Jeremy—rubber ears and all.

"Gross. You really know how to whet a customer's appetite," said Ginger, warily eyeing her hamburger before picking it up and taking a bite.

"So," she said, washing down the burger with a sip of iced tea, "how did the funeral go?"

"You must have been the only person in town who wasn't there," Kendra remarked.

Ginger shrugged. "What can I say, funerals aren't the most fun thing for me."

"Well, it was kinda strange," Aunt Jewel answered. "It started out like any normal funeral, then Mrs. Bunch's son came staggerin' in drunk as a skunk, mumblin' and stumblin' around."

Kendra glanced up at Jeremy. "Thanks to Big-Ears Avenger here, we know that he was mumbling something about 'loving a cake'."

"What?" Ginger asked, laughing.

"Ask him," Kendra nodded in Jeremy's direction.

He frowned, shrugged, and looked down at the checkerboard tile floor. "That's what it sounded like, anyway."

"Now you're not sure?" Kendra asked.

"No. Not really. Look, it didn't make any sense, 'k? He was mumbling and whispering. I don't really know what he said. Sorry."

Kendra grimaced and hacked away at her steak. "Great."

Aunt Jewel thought for a minute. "But did you see Pastor Holt's face when Harry stumbled in? It was as white as a ghost's sheets on laundry day. I wonder if they know each other? Their reaction was definitely strange."

"Hers, too?" Kendra asked. "I didn't notice that," she said, surprised. "I was too busy staring at Harry when he made his entrance to notice what the pastor was doing. Speaking of ghosts, I did manage to take some photos of the cemetery there the other night, and got some very strange vibes from the good pastor and his wife."

"Gee, sounds like y'all had a wonderful time. I'm sorry I couldn't make it," Ginger commented wryly.

"Yeah, right. Looks like you're pert near eaten up with remorse," Jewel commented.

"Well," Ginger defended herself. "I never liked the old . . .Mrs. Bunch. Even back in high school, she was a terror. Nobody liked her."

"That's right," Jewel said. "I'd forgotten she

used to teach English here at the high school. Then when she retired, she took it all on herself to get the library started and solicited donations from the citizens for it."

"So she actually started the library?" Kendra asked, surprised.

"Yeah, she did. Whatever you want to say about the woman, she has done some good things for this town," Jewel said.

Ginger spoke up. "The problem with Mrs. Bunch was that she didn't know when to let go. Sarah told me that she had tried repeatedly to get Nora fired. But the board voted against it. They know a good thing when they got it."

"You're right. Nora's probably the best thing that ever happened to the Nameless Public Library," Jewel agreed.

"That woman certainly works like a demon. She's going to school at U.T. to get her Master's in Library Science—with her job and two kids, to boot," Ginger added.

"She's also working on the church library. At least, they want her to. I saw her last night over at the church when I went to take some photos."

"Oh yeah," Ginger said. "So how did that go?"

Kendra groaned. "Oh. It went all right. Let's just say it was quite bizarre. There was something strange going on over there."

"What happened?" Jewel asked.

Kendra fiddled with her straw. "To be honest, I'm not really sure what's going on over there. I heard some loud voices, some strange noises, then I saw them, uh, making out and kissing."

"In the church?" Ginger squealed.

Kendra nodded.

"How strange," Jewel said. "I hear the church is having trouble paying the bills."

Kendra took a sip of her tea and nodded. "Yeah, there's that, too. She did mention how low the pastor's salary is."

"I don't know what they're moanin' about money for," Aunt Jewel interjected. "Looks like they're got plenty of it. Verna Holt dresses fit to kill. Did you get a look at that outfit she was wearin' to the funeral? And that preacher doesn't look too shabby himself. Did you get a load of that diamond tie tack he was wearin'?"

Jeremy, eavesdropping as usual, perched on the back of the circular booth. "That thing almost blinded me when it caught the light."

"And that brooch! Whooee! It was a beauty!" Jewel said.

"She said she inherited it," Kendra explained. "She told me that she couldn't afford things like that on his salary. She got almost defensive and preachy about it when I admired it. She claims the church's contributions are down this year." Kendra took another bite of her chicken fried steak. "Umm. Good." She swallowed. "By the way, I spoke to Nora after the meeting. I asked her about that list of books."

"What did she say?" Jewel asked.

Kendra shrugged. "Not much. Just that the titles are books that are controversial, or that have been banned from area school libraries recently."

"We knew that," Jeremy quipped.

"Yeah. All except for *Love's Wild Embrace*."

Ginger nodded. "Right. That one is curious."

"Looks like she wanted it removed from the library," Jeremy ventured.

"You don't suppose . . ." Ginger started.

"What?" Kendra asked.

"You don't suppose Mrs. Bunch wrote that book, do you?"

Jewel hooted. "That old windbag? Shoot, I'd be more likely to write something like that than she would."

Kendra grinned. "So, Aunt Jewel. What have you been doing with your free time lately?"

"No, dear. I didn't write that book anymore than . . . than . . .well, than Buster Briggs did."

"What's that about the sheriff?" Jim asked, tossing his hat on the seat behind him and sliding into the large corner booth beside Kendra.

"Uh, nothing," Kendra laughed. "So, you made it after all."

"Nuthin' much goin' on over at the office. Besides, Sheriff Briggs likes me to hang out with you."

Kendra cocked an eyebrow. "Oh, he does, does he?"

"Yep. Well, actually, he told me to keep an eye on your Aunt Jewel here. And since y'all are around each other so much, well, you know how dedicated I am to my job." He grinned.

"Right," Kendra smiled. "So, has the sheriff come up with any new leads?"

"Nope. To tell the truth, he's not really lookin' for any. He's pretty sure your auntie here did not bonk Mrs. Bunch over the head, though."

"I wondered why he hasn't arrested me yet. He acted like he was so all-fired sure it was me," Jewel said.

"He knows where you live, and he figures you ain't gonna go anywhere." He looked around and lowered his voice. "And just between us, he thinks the real killer will get cocky and make a mistake if he thinks we already have a suspect."

"Eeep!" Jewel choked and took a sip of tea. "So, basically, I'm a guinea pig. He wants me to lure the real killer out into the open. Is that right?"

Jim smiled. "I'm afraid so."

Kendra frowned. "That's just what I figured. We'll just have to keep asking questions on our own until we come up with some answers."

"What do you mean, keep askin' questions on your own?" Jim frowned. "Kendra Louise Harper, if I find out you've been playing cop . . ."

Kendra looked down at her plate and toyed with the remainder of her food. Jeremy looked up at the ceiling and started whistling.

"OK, you two—spill the beans. What have y'all gone and done that I oughta know about?" the deputy asked, folding his arms over his chest. "Go ahead. I'm listenin'."

"Well," Jeremy started, "you know we're all worried about Aunt Jewel here. I've just been keeping my ears on around here in case I hear something pertinent to the investigation."

"So to speak," said Ginger.

"And I," Kendra explained, "have only asked Nora about that list of books Mrs. Bunch had on her when she died. That's all . . .really." So far, she thought.

"That's all, huh?" Jim said. "I know I don't have to remind you that there's a killer loose around here. You could get him or her mighty riled up, if you keep goin' around askin' lots of questions. I don't want you messed up in this, Kendra."

She stared at him. "It's a little late for that, isn't it?"

"We'll be careful," Jeremy said. "We know how to be subtle at our information gathering, don't we, Kendra?"

She stared at his pointy pink rubber ears, his currently coal black spiky hair, his purple neon tie-dyed shirt and his one pierced ear from which dangled a cluster of iridescent purple beads.

"No comment," she finally said.

The cafe was quiet for a moment then Jewel spoke. "Jim, what do you know about Eula-Mae's son?"

He shrugged. "Not much, really. We've checked him out, but we didn't find anything. Harry Bunch played football in high school then enrolled in U.T. majoring in business. He made good grades, but after a while he dropped out and got a job here in Nameless workin' for the city."

"Doing what?" Kendra asked.

"Not much, apparently. Supposedly, he got fired after about a year, moved back home with his mother and started drinkin' pretty heavily."

"That's it?" Jewel asked.

"Yep. 'Fraid so. Look, I wish as much as y'all do that we had more to go on, but we don't." He patted Jewel's hand. "Just hold on. We're bound to get a break on the case sooner or later. Even though Sheriff Brigg's attentions are elsewhere, I want you to know that I'm doin' all I can to get your name officially cleared."

"Thanks, Jim. I appreciate that," she answered.

"Well, ready to go, Kendra? I'm really lookin' forward to seein' that movie."

"What movie?" Aunt Jewel asked.

Kendra smiled mysteriously as she slid out of the booth. "We haven't decided yet."

CHAPTER NINE

Jim followed Kendra to her house and rushed over to open the door of her car for her. He stood aside impatiently while she unlocked the front door and flipped on a few lights.

"Want some coffee?" she asked, her head inside the refrigerator. "Or some wine?"

"Umm, some wine would be nice," he answered, pulling his shoes off and propping his feet up on her sofa table.

She sat down beside him and immediately, Boo the cat jumped up on her lap, giving her a head butt.

"Jim?"

"Hmm, babe?" he murmured, moving over to nuzzle her ear.

Kendra swatted him away like an annoying fly. "Did y'all happen to find any fingerprints on the jar?"

He stopped nuzzling and frowned. "Kendra, come on. Let's forget about the murder for a few hours, OK? I'm ready to relax."

"Did you?"

Jim blew out a breath. "No fingerprints. We did find a few fibers stuck to several of the glass pieces, though."

"What kind of fibers?"

"They were a mixture, really. Mostly cotton, but some wool and polyester."

"Oh great! What a *big* clue!" she said sarcastically. "Everybody at the workshop was wearing either cotton or polyester. And we were practically drowning in wool!"

"Now calm down. You've been watching too many TV cop shows, Kendra. We don't have a huge crime lab here. Hell, we don't have *any* crime lab here. We do our best, and we're still checking on a few things. As far as I'm concerned, this investigation has just started. Don't worry. Your aunt's not goin' to jail. Not if I can help it."

He pulled her back against him and started rubbing her shoulders. "Now just relax. That's it," he whispered into her ear.

"Jim?"

"Umm?"

"We forgot to rent a movie."

"Yeah, I know." He grinned wickedly and shrugged. "We'll just have to find something else to do."

"Oh no, you don't," she said, gave him a peck on the cheek and jumped up. "I have work to do, and so do you. I'll see you later, OK?"

He sighed. "Sure, Kendra. But eventually, we have to have a talk about the two of us."

She smiled, pulled him up off the sofa and gently pushed him towards the door. "Goodnight,

Jim. I'll talk to you tomorrow."

He finally consented to go, and Kendra stood at the door frowning until his taillights on his truck had disappeared down the street.

She checked the back porch light, locked the door then fell into bed with a book about Texas graveyard ghosts.

The next morning, while the coffee was brewing, Kendra went into her office and took out the notes she'd made for her library presentation. She remembered the photos she'd taken and made a mental note to download them the next chance she got.

"Coffee's done, Aunt Jewel!" she called. "Want some? I'll bring it in to you if you want."

Jewel stumbled into the kitchen, her hair sticking up straight on one side and her eyes looked baggy and tired. She wore a voluminous house dress with pearl snaps down the front.

"You were up late," she said. "Jim here?"

Kendra looked at her aunt. "Nope. He was here last night, but left early. I had work to do. I'm stressing out about that library presentation, and I know I shouldn't."

Jewel shrugged. "It's your first time, honey. You're bound to have a few raw nerves about it. I'm sure it'll be fine. You know your material and love what you're doing."

Kendra nodded. "Yeah, that's true. But I wish I had more time to prepare."

"Why didn't you tell them you need more time in the first place?"

"I couldn't do that. I'm still new in town compared to some, and I want to make a good impression. They want it done around Halloween for their anniversary celebration. Besides, I need the money from this, you know that."

"Not that they're paying much," Aunt Jewel sniffed.

"You're right about that. But that's not the point," she hesitated. "Not the whole point, anyway. I probably would have done it for free. Don't tell Nora, though." She smiled. "You know how much I love talking about local folklore and ghost stories."

"Honey, I hate to bring it up, but why don't you try to get a job? I mean, working for somebody else. You could teach or something. You're drivin' yourself crazy tryin' to make a living, writing the occasional essay here and there, doing research for folks."

"Folklorists historically have not been rich, Aunt Jewel," she said quietly. "I'm not in it for the money." She snorted, frustrated. "Right. A real job? As in 9-to-5? Doin' what? Programming computers? Brain surgery? Or maybe I'll apply to be an astronaut." She turned away, tears brimming in her eyes.

108

"Honey, look at me," Jewel said, turning Kendra towards her. "I'm sorry. Just forget I said that. I know you love what you do, but at some point you gotta face the music. You're barely scrapin' by here. I'm willing to support you as much as I can, but I don't really have much of an income, either."

Kendra nodded. "I know, and I really appreciate it that you took me in when I needed a place to stay. You are right about that barely scraping by thing. Once this thing with Mrs. Bunch is solved, I'm planning to do some more workshops, and there's that book proposal that hasn't been rejected yet. I suppose I could always help Nora out at the library if I get desperate. I still have some of my savings."

"Look, never mind I said anything. We've got enough on your mind right now. We'll do OK," Jewel said.

"What I need is a fairy godmother," Kendra said.

Jewel laughed. "Don't we all?"

Kendra felt guilty, but she was almost glad when Aunt Jewel left later on to meet up with some friends at the diner for lunch. They were plotting some kind of new garden project that she was excited about.

Kendra trudged back upstairs to her loft, all of a sudden not feeling up to working on the presentation. Instead, she sat down and started researching some new ideas for her next book, a collection of local ghost stories.

Kendra breathed a sigh of relief when the phone rang and she heard Ginger's voice. "Hey there! Feel up to taking a ride out to the country to count some sheep?"

"What are you talking about?" Kendra asked.

"The Martins are shearing their sheep today, and they've invited us out to check it out."

Kendra hesitated, thinking she should stay at home and work. Then she thought better of it. "It might be a good opportunity to talk to the sisters. Maybe they saw something that would help Aunt Jewel."

"Good! I'll be over in a few minutes to pick you up."

Kendra hung up the phone and ran to get her camera. She wanted to take some photos of the sheep shearing for a possible chapter in the book she wanted to write about weaving and spinning lore. She searched in the loft and living room for her camera, but couldn't find it. She frowned, trying to remember where she had it last. Had she downloaded the last set of photos, and if so, where had she put the camera after doing that? She went back upstairs to the loft, searched some more, but still couldn't find it.

She was searching in the kitchen when Ginger came to the back door. "Got any coffee?" she asked, opening the cabinet and grabbing a ceramic mug.

"Yeah, sure. Help yourself," Kendra said, tossing the sofa cushions to the floor.

"Lose something?" Ginger asked, glancing over she shoulder.

"Yeah, my danged camera! I know I had it here a few days ago, because I downloaded a set of photos." She frowned, looking around the room. "But I can't seem to find it now. I swear! The smaller the house, the more trouble it is for me to find things!"

Ginger helped her search for a few minutes. No camera. "Was that before or after you took those photos at the church?"

"Oh, I don't know! I feel like I'm losing my friggin' mind lately. I think it was after." She thought for a moment, then shook her head. "Never mind," Kendra said. "I'll find it later. It couldn't have gone far."

"Don't worry, I've got mine in the car. I'll help you look for it again when we get back."

Kendra frowned, took one last look around the room, and shrugged. "OK, that'll work." She grabbed her notebook and purse and locked the door behind her, glancing one last time around the room, wondering where in the hell she'd put her camera.

CHAPTER TEN

Kendra loved going out to the Martin's farm; it felt as comfortable to her as an old pair of shoes. The farmhouse itself was a big, rambling two-story painted a chalky white with dark green trim. The tin roof was rusted in spots, but it still did the job. A wide covered porch ran along the front of the house, shading the inside from the hot Texas sun. A cedar swing creaked back and forth in the breeze. A bright red rose twined up and across the porch railing, and fat honeybees bounced among the bright pink potted geraniums that lined the steps. A fat orange cat was draped across the railing, his ears twitching.

As Ginger drove up to the Martin's house, Mrs. Martin came out onto the front porch, grinning and wiping her hands on her faded calico apron, waving to them.

"Well my goodness!" she called. "Look what the cat drug in. Y'all come on up here. The shearin's about to start. But there's no hurry, we've got lots of sheep to do today. Y'all have time for a cup of coffee or glass of ice-tea first, don't you?"

Oma and Alma Martin's mother, Flora, was about the same age as Aunt Jewel, but time hadn't treated her as kindly. Her skin was weathered and crinkly as aged parchment, no doubt from the hours she had spent in the winter cold and the summer heat tending to her flock of black-faced sheep. With her apron and gingham dress, Kendra thought that her plump pink cheeks made her look like a wizened apple-head doll. Flora Martin stepped off the porch and met Kendra and Ginger, wrapping them both up into a ferocious hug.

"Kendra, how's your Aunt Jewel gettin' along these days? My girls told me about the ruckus you had there at your workshop. They've been spooked ever since. It's a pity that you can't go nowhere these days without runnin' into meanness. I tell you it's everwhere."

"Jewel's fine," Kendra answered. "She's getting a little frustrated that no real leads have turned up on the real murderer, though. But in general, she's OK."

Flora shook her head, holding open the wooden screen door so they could go into the house. "And I don't suppose our good sheriff is doin' much about it, is he?"

"Well . . ." Kendra started.

"As a matter of fact, Mrs. Martin, he's not," Ginger interrupted, following her into the kitchen. "If it weren't for Deputy Wyman, I think the sheriff would have already locked up Aunt Jewel and washed his hands of the whole mess."

"That's what I thought," Mrs. Martin admitted, nodding. "It's a good thing you've got

113

that handsome young deputy on your side, Kendra. Aren't y'all scared that the real murderer will come back?"

Kendra shook her head. "No, not really. We're pretty sure that whoever killed Mrs. Bunch was specifically after her, killed her in the heat of the moment. I don't think we have to worry about them coming back. At least, I hope not."

Mrs. Martin nodded. "You're probably right about that. That woman could turn a saint into a devil with just one look. I'm sorry she's dead, I suppose, but I'm not surprised that someone killed her. She sure had a nasty way about her at times. That woman had a mean streak the size of the Guadalupe."

"Yeah, that's what we've noticed," Ginger said. "We've both had a few run-ins with her over the years."

Kendra and Ginger sat down at the long pine table in the kitchen while Flora poured them cups of coffee in large handmade pottery mugs.

"I know that your daughters have had trouble with Mrs. Bunch in the past, and I know about the unfortunate incident with your ewe . . ." Kendra started.

"Raincloud."

"Excuse me?" Kendra asked, glancing out the window of the kitchen.

"Raincloud. Her name was Raincloud," Flora said.

114

"Oh, yes. Raincloud. Anyway, we know about all that, and we're sorry. But is there anything else you can tell us about Eula-Mae that might help us?"

"Are you investigating the murder?" she asked.

"Not really," Kendra said. "But there's a possibility that Aunt Jewel will be arrested, and we're trying to nip that in the bud."

Flora Martin pursed her lips and looked thoughtful. "Well, there's the garden club thing. That was quite a big hoo-hah."

"We heard something about that. What exactly happened?" Ginger asked.

"Well, Mrs. High-and-Mighty Bunch didn't want my girls to be in her garden club. I'm not sure why, except that maybe she thought they would cause trouble for her over the death of Raincloud. And she's probably right about that. Anyway, she voted against their membership, and the other members followed her lead like a bunch of . . ."

"Sheep?" Ginger said.

"Yeah," Flora grinned. "Like a bunch of sheep. Eula-Mae's middle name should have been 'Railroad' because of the way she pushes the other members around. She always has to have her own way, never thinking about what others might want. Of course the girls got their feelins' hurt, and didn't say anything else about the club after that. But they were sure anxious to join at first—real excited about it." She looked out the window for a second. "My girls are loners who spend too much time hangin' around here with me and the sheep. I was real happy when they decided to join the club and be around other people for a change."

Kendra nodded as she sipped her coffee. "Anything else you can tell us about Mrs. Bunch?"

"Well, I suppose you know about the rumors, so I won't bore you talkin' about those. That's all old news anyway."

"What rumors?" Kendra and Ginger asked simultaneously.

"Why, the rumors about Mrs. Bunch's son, Harry, and that Holt woman."

"The pastor's wife?" Kendra asked.

Mrs. Martin nodded.

"What happened?" Kendra asked.

"Well, the way I heard it was that Mrs. Holt took a shine to Mrs. Bunch's son, Harry, and set out to get him."

"What do you mean 'get him'? In what way?"

Flora snorted. "Why, in bed of course. Or in the back of a truck, or the hayloft, up against the tombstones in the cemetery or anywhere else she could, I reckon." She chuckled and glanced over at Kendra. "Can you imagine those two together?"

Kendra shook her head.

116

"Are you sure about this? This is the same Verna Holt that we know?" Ginger asked. "The preacher's wife?"

"Yes ma'am. The same one. She was quite the little hellcat, pardon my French, when she was younger."

"I just can't believe it," Kendra said.

"I know. It's hard to believe, ain't it? Anyway, Mrs. Bunch found out about it and told Harry to stay away from her, or else. Gotta give her that."

"Or else what?"

"She threatened to tell Pastor Holt that his wife and Harry were diddlin' around."

"What a rotten thing for a mother to do to her own son!" Ginger exclaimed.

"Well, that was Mrs. Eula-Mae Bunch all over again. She was an evil person through and through. I doubt if many in town care that she's dead."

Kendra nodded. "Yeah, it's starting to look like you're right about that. So then what happened?" Kendra asked.

Flora Martin shrugged. "Not much, I guess. Supposedly he never went near her again. He didn't want to cause trouble for her. Whatever they say about Harry Bunch, he realized he was playing with fire and backed off."

"Sounds like," Kendra agreed.

"But is this story really true?" Ginger asked.

"Who knows? I myself find it mighty hard to believe, I must say. Well, drink up your coffee, girls. The sheep are waitin'."

After several hours of watching the Martin sisters wrestle sheep to the ground and shearing them, and after the last sheep was running around in the pasture, looking humiliated, naked and much thinner, Kendra decided she'd had enough of the dust and the heat for one day. Ginger said she was ready to go home, too.

They loaded two fleece into the back of Ginger's truck and thanked the Martins for inviting them out to the farm. Ginger liked to buy her spinning wool locally, directly from the producer, and she had never been disappointed with the quality of the Martin's wool. Kendra was looking forward to helping her clean the wool. She found the whole process of washing the wool to be soothing and calming. The Martins kept their sheep fairly clean, compared to some. Kendra thought she could do with a bit of calm, given the past few days.

As Kendra and Ginger drove home, they talked about what Mrs. Martin had said about Mrs. Holt and Harry Bunch.

"I still can't believe that Verna Holt and Harry Bunch were sleepin' together," Ginger mused. "But you never know, do you?"

Kendra grinned. "I'm with Mrs. Martin—I can't even imagine those two together."

"Me either," Ginger agreed. "I wonder if she wore her pillbox hats to their . . . assignations."

Kendra laughed. "Maybe she did! Even if they did have *assignations*, I doubt it has anything to do with Mrs. Bunch's murder. I mean, that had to have been years ago. Right?"

"Right," Ginger said, pulling the truck into Kendra's driveway. "But you never know . . . Oh no! What now?"

"What's wrong?" Kendra asked.

Ginger was staring at the street in front of Kendra's house. It was littered with the trash from her two metal trashcans. The two cans that were lying in the middle of the road, flat as pancakes.

CHAPTER ELEVEN

Sheriff Buster Briggs pulled up in front of Kendra's house in his cruiser just as she and Ginger had finished gathering up the trash from the street and stuffing it into a plastic bag.

"Good grief, not him again," Kendra groaned under her breath. "This is all I need today. Mr. Adams probably turned me in for littering."

They watched as the sheriff uncoiled himself from the car, carefully positioned his Stetson on his head, and turned towards them.

Ginger frowned. "Why is it that I feel guilty every time I just look at that man? And I haven't even done anything wrong!"

"I know what you mean. He makes me feel the same way. God, I hope he's not here to arrest Aunt Jewel."

They watched as the sheriff nodded to them without a word and turned towards Jack Adams' house next door.

"Whew!" Kendra said. "That was close. But I wonder why he's talking to Mr. Nosy again. Surely he'd told him all he knows by now."

"Which is nothing, if you ask me." With a worried glance at the house next door, Kendra and Ginger went inside.

"Sheriff Briggs, nice to see you again!" Jack Adams shouted as he opened the front door. "Come in, come in. Make yourself at home."

The sheriff coiled into the end of the sofa, twirling his hat between his hands and looked around the room.

"Would you like a drink?" Mr. Adams chattered nervously. "I have iced tea, Coke, or maybe a beer? What the heck, it's after noon."

The sheriff stared at Mr. Adams, unblinking. "On duty," he finally said.

"Well, maybe not. Of course not. Silly me. You're on duty. Stupid of me." He took a deep breath. "So, Sheriff Briggs, what brings you over here?"

The sheriff stared at the man for a moment before answering. "Just checkin' on a few things, that's all."

"Uh, what things?" Mr. Adams answered nervously.

"For instance, you said you saw Miz Bunch and Miz Moore arguing at the gate next door before Miz Bunch was killed."

Mr. Adams' head bobbed. "That's right, I did."

"What was she wearing?"
"What? Who?"

121

"Mrs. Moore. What was she wearing?"

"Um, well, I already told you, didn't I? It was a . . . kind of a . . .dark thing. A dark dress."

The sheriff pulled out a small notebook and a stubby pencil. "What color dress?" he asked.

"Uh, what color? I already told you. It was dark . . .blue. Or green. Or red."

The sheriff slowly pushed his notebook and pencil back in his pocket. "I see. Mr. Adams. So it was blue. Or green. Or red. Earlier I believe you said it was definitely blue. Did you not?"

Mr. Adams swallowed noisily. "Uh, well. I can't really be sure." He laughed nervously. "I mean . . . I'm positive it was Mrs. Moore who killed Eula-Mae. I saw her. What difference does it make what color dress she was wearing?"

The sheriff sprang up from the sofa and clapped his hat on his head in one smooth motion. "No difference at all, Mr. Adams, I'm afraid. We'll be in touch if we need anything further from you."

"Uh, when are you going to arrest her then, sheriff?"

"I'm not going to arrest her, Mr. Adams."

"What?"

"I said I'm not. There's no real evidence that she did anything. All we got on this case is one dead body. No fingerprints, no evidence, no nuthin'. And we had a whole herd of women over there trampling all over the crime scene. If we had a reliable witness, it might be different, but . . ."

Mr. Adams' face turned red. "But what?" he sputtered. "A reliable witness? But sheriff, I know what I saw and . . ."

Sheriff Briggs raised his hand and silenced him with one look. "What you saw, Mr. Adams, was a whole lot of nothin'. Nothin' useful to this investigation, that is. You can't even know what color dress the woman was wearin'."

The sheriff shook his head and walked out onto the front porch. "I suggest you don't waste anymore of my time. Unless you come up with some concrete facts to back your claims."

Before Mr. Adams could answer, the sheriff was gone.

"Why that dirty . . ." he whispered, staring over at Kendra's house. He shuffled over to the telephone and punched in a number. After a few seconds, he started speaking. "Yeah, it's me. All of a sudden, our fine sheriff doesn't believe my story." He paused to listen for several seconds. "I'm sorry, I want no part of this. I've done what I can, and it's all been for nothing. Don't you threaten me! I did what you asked. Now it's over." He slammed the receiver back into the cradle, his face turning a very unbecoming color.

After Ginger left, Kendra went up to her loft office to work. A couple of minutes later, the doorbell rang. For a second, she decided to ignore it then groaned, ran down and pulled open the door. Verna Holt stood on the porch, all smiles. She was dressed impeccably, like always, in a crisp two-piece suit and gloves. A pillbox hat perched on her head.

"Kendra, I was in the area and just thought I'd pop over and see how your Aunt Jewel is doing. Just my Christian duty, you understand. Is she home?" she asked, pushing her way into the living room. "You don't mind if I come in for a bit, do you? It's so blamed hot out there." She looked around. "My, my, you've really done a lot to this house since you moved in with your Aunt Jewel. It looks nice."

"Thank you," Kendra said. "It's been a lot of hard work, but worth it. I'm afraid my aunt isn't here right now. She's out with a few of her friends and won't be back for a while. Is there something I can do for you?"

"Well, no, not really. I just thought I'd stop by. This nasty business with the murder and all has got everybody nervous as cats, you see."

"Yes, well, the sheriff is handling it," Kendra said, thinking about what Mrs. Martin had said about Verna and Harry Bunch having an affair. She still found it hard to believe.

"Of course he is, bless his heart," Verna said. "As he should. It is his job, after all. Although, I just have to wonder, given the way things are these days, all the meanness in the world . . ."

Kendra frowned. "I don't understand. You have to wonder what, exactly?"

Verna shrugged. "Oh, well, frankly, if we have a maniac running around town? The thought of it just makes me sick to think of it!" She swooned a bit, and Kendra led her to the sofa.

"Why don't you sit down here for a minute; I'll go get you a glass of water."

"That would be wonderful, dear. It's hotter than H.E. double-toothpicks out there."

Kendra grinned as she walked into the kitchen and got a glass of water for Mrs. Holt. She walked back into the living room and handed the glass to the woman. "There you go. Nice and cold."

"Yes, dear, thank you!" Verna said, gulping the water. "I really appreciate it, and God does, too! When you give a good Christian a drink of cold water, you give God a drink!" She quickly rose to leave, almost turning the glass over. "You tell your Aunt Jewel that I came by and that I'm prayin' for her."

Kendra nodded. "Uh, sure thing."

"I must be going now. I have lots of work to do over at the church." Mrs. Holt hurried towards the door. "I'll be in touch, dear. Bye now," she said, leaving abruptly.

Kendra shook her head as she closed the f door. She was finding it harder and harder to believe the rumors about Mrs. Holt and Harry

125

Bunch. She didn't know Harry, but Verna just did not seem like the type.

In spite of herself, though, she smiled at the naughty image that came unbidden to her mind. She remembered what Mrs. Martin said about Verna and the tombstones. Kendra turned to go back up into the loft. Out of the corner of her eye, she noticed something dark on the floor next to the end of the sofa. "What the hell?" she said and stopped in her tracks. Her camera was on the floor at the end of the sofa—in plain sight. OK, now this was just weird. Kendra tried again to remember the last time she'd used it. At the church? She distinctly remembered putting it in the front seat of the truck before going back to the parking lot to speak with Nora. She shook her head, wondering if she was going crazy.

Finding her camera reminded Kendra of the photo files she took at the church. She still hadn't looked at them. She grabbed a glass of iced tea and ran upstairs to her office, anxious to see if any of the nighttime shots were clear enough to use. She printed out a handful of her favorites, trying to decide which she'd use in her Halloween presentation at the library. Kendra sat in the dark flipping through the photos. The ones taken in the sanctuary were a bit dark, but she knew with a little tweaking, they would be fine. The outdoor shots were full of atmosphere, dark, and creepy. She smiled. They were perfect for the Halloween presentation! As she finished the set and closed the file, Kendra frowned as an image flashed through her memory. She snatched at it, but it was gone as soon as it appeared. "Damn!" she muttered.

All night long, something nagged at the back of her mind. Something not quite right. But as hard as she tried, Kendra couldn't figure out what it was.

CHAPTER TWELVE

From her front window, Kendra watched Deputy Jim Wyman take a large bouquet of sunflowers from the back seat of his cruiser. He knew how much she loved the bright yellows and greens of the flowers, and had managed to get her a bunch every summer since they'd met three years ago. Never mind that their yard was full of flowers, including sunflowers. She smiled. It was the thought that counted.

A sudden feeling of irritation washed over her as she watched him struggle simultaneously with the bouquet and the car door. Kendra didn't understand it; she wasn't sure why she should be irritated at Jim. He was the sweetest, kindest and most considerate man she'd ever met. And he was, according to her Aunt Jewel and all of her friends, madly in love with her. Maybe that was the problem. Kendra knew he was in love with her; Ginger and Sarah knew he was in love with her; Aunt Jewel knew it and for God's sake even Virginia knew he was in love with her! It seemed that the deputy was the only one in town who didn't have a clue. She still hadn't decided how she felt about him, though. She definitely loved him, but she'd been burned before and was wary of getting into another relationship.

As Jim walked through the garden gate and up the path to the door, he whistled. Kendra watched him juggle the flowers and a mysterious package, and her irritation turned to a warm feeling that she even had trouble putting a name to. She did *love* him. She just wasn't sure she was *in love* with him. Where was the great passion that she expected? Where were the undying professions of love? Maybe her expectations were too high.

Kendra hastily wiped the tears away that were trickling down all of a sudden. She shook her head as if to dislodge the thoughts that were hovering there, and forced a bright smile on her face.

She creaked open the screen door, meeting Jim as he walked up onto the porch. "For me?" she said, taking the bouquet and turning her face up to his for a hasty kiss.

"Of course they're for you, Sunshine," he said, coming into the house. As soon as the door was closed, he pulled her into his arms for a longer, lingering kiss.

"Mr. Adams is lurking about outside," he murmured. "I feel like we're under siege in here."

Kendra laughed, her former gloomy mood vanquished for the moment. Sunflowers always did cheer her up. She took the flowers to the kitchen and put them into a large blue enamel antique coffee pot filled with water. As she turned

129

to place them on the living room table, someone began pounding on the front door.

"Oh, no! I hope that's not who I think it is," she said.

Jim peeked out the front window. "Speak of the devil. Yep, it's him, and he looks like he's loaded for bear."

Kendra groaned as she jerked the door open.

"Mr. Adams. What do you want?" she asked rudely.

He craned his neck around her until he spotted Jim. "Ah ha! Cavorting with the enemy, are we? Seems like a conflict of interest to me, deputy."

Kendra seethed. "If you don't get off of my property this instant, I'll . . ."

"You'll do what, missy? Knock me over the head with a glass jar full of vile blue stuff, just like your Aunt Jewel did to poor old Mrs. Bunch?"

"How dare you!" Kendra said.

"Whoa, there, you two," Jim interrupted, striding to the door and firmly putting Kendra behind himself. "Mr. Adams. It's really none of your business what I do with my free time. And furthermore, Mrs. Moore has not been arrested for any crime, and she won't be, either. I believe the sheriff told you that, did he not? I think you should apologize to Ms. Harper here and go peacefully back over to your own house."

"Now listen here, young man! Just because

you're standing there in that fancy brown uniform of yours doesn't mean I have to take orders from you. I take my orders from Sheriff Briggs and nobody else!"

Jim crossed his arms over his chest. "Well, then. I happen to know that Sheriff Briggs already told you that you're an unreliable witness and that your so-called eyewitness account of the murder isn't worth a hill of beans!

Mr. Adams sputtered and his face turned red. "Well, I never!" He peered into the house at Kendra, squinting. "This isn't over, Miss Harper. Not by a long shot. I saw what I saw and I'm not changin' my story now."

"Oh, I would if I were you," Jim said.

"What? Why?" He sputtered.

Jim help up one finger. "Number one. I'm not wearing a brown uniform. This shirt is dark green and the pants are plain old blue jeans. It seems you're having a little trouble distinguishing colors, Mr. Adams. So you really can't be sure who you saw kill Mrs. Bunch, much less what color they were wearing."

He held up a second finger. "And two. I've checked our records, and it has come to my attention that you seem to have quite a number of unpaid traffic citations for various things here in town. Illegal parking, running a red light in the middle of downtown, and bashing into the stop sign at the corner of Second and Wall Streets. You know, I bet I could pull your license right now if I weren't off-duty."

Jack Adams sputtered. "Why, the nerve!"

Jim smiled. "What do ya' think, Mr. Adams? Time to go home?"

He peered at the two of them and turned to leave. Kendra pushed Jim aside and called to Mr. Adams.

"And by the way, you owe us for one indigo bush and two metal trash cans. I figure one-hundred-dollars should just about cover it."

Mr. Adams turned and scowled at Kendra. He opened his mouth to speak then clamped it shut. He nodded briefly then walked slowly towards his own house. Several times he turned back to look at them, peering and squinting. "This isn't over!" he yelled.

Kendra shook her head as she slammed the door. "Little weasel. I swear, that man reminds me of Mr. Magoo the way he peers at everyone."

"Who?" Jim asked.

"Mr. Magoo! You know, the cartoon character who couldn't see? He was blind as a bat."

"Ah, right," he said, nodding, "Now I remember. You know, Mr. Adams probably doesn't realize it, but without any doubt, he just gave us another really good reason not to arrest your aunt for Eula-Mae's murder."

Kendra nodded. "That's right. Why, the man's half blind. He's at least color blind. He's proven that himself. Do you think Sheriff Briggs will leave Aunt Jewel alone if you tell him what just happened here?"

Jim grinned. "I don't have to. I talked to the sheriff before I came over here, and he's already decided your aunt is innocent. He's already said Jack Adams is an unreliable witness."

"Really? She's cleared? Officially?"

Jim nodded. "Yep. Looks like."

"That's great news! Let me call her and tell her."

Jim grabbed Kendra around the waist. "Can't that wait a little while?" he murmured as he nuzzled her neck.

Kendra's eyes twinkled as she squirmed away. "Stop that—it tickles!" She giggled. "I suppose I can call her later."

"Good girl," Jim murmured as he dipped his head for a kiss. He paused and frowned. "By the way, how did you know Adams ran over your trashcans?"

Kendra shrugged. "I really didn't. It was just a bluff, a lucky guess. Who else could have done it?"

Jim threw back his head and laughed. "Good one! Remind me never to play poker with you."

"Not even strip poker?" she teased, leading him down the hallway. "I'll get the cards."

133

Several hours later, Kendra sat curled up on the end of the sofa, staring at the ceiling. Jim had wanted to stay all night, but she gently pushed him out the door, explaining that she really had a lot of work to do. When Aunt Jewel got home later, she told her what Sheriff Briggs and Jim had decided about Mr. Adams' poor eyesight. They made plans to go to Do-Lolly's Diner for breakfast the next morning to celebrate, then they both went to bed.

Kendra took a deep breath as she relaxed and began to doze off. Everything was going to be all right. Her aunt was no longer a suspect and things could get back to normal. Kendra breathed a sigh of relief and fell into a deep slumber.

Sometime during the night, Kendra began playing out the events of the dye workshop in a dream.

She saw Eula-Mae Bunch walking in the courtyard gate, and behind her trotted a bevy of properly dressed members of the Nameless Garden Club.

Next in line came the Martin sisters, Alma and Oma, with Verna Holt trailing behind. Alma and Oma were leading a sheep on a leash. The librarian, Nora Rogers, walked in carrying a stack of books. Although she couldn't read the titles, Kendra knew they were the ones on the list found in Eula-Mae's pocket.

Jewel, Ginger and Sarah were standing on the front porch, watching the silent crowd filter by.

134

Suddenly Jim, Sheriff Briggs and Jack Adams appeared at the gate. The sheriff slammed the gate and suddenly it became a metal grate, like a pair of prison doors.

Mr. Adams pointed at Aunt Jewel and said, "I saw her. She killed Mrs. Bunch."

The deputy walked towards her aunt with a pair of handcuffs. A shot rang out from somewhere, and Kendra screamed "No!" and sat up in bed, wide awake.

She took a deep breath and wiped the perspiration from her brow with the back of her hand.

"Wow, must be a delayed reaction," she murmured, and shakily got out of bed and went to the kitchen for a glass of water. As she drank, she stared out the window over the sink into the blackness. The street was quiet at this time of night. She saw the taillights of a car as it raced through the corner stop sign, not bothering to stop. She shook her head.

Kendra wandered around the eat-in kitchen and as she passed the dining table, she noticed the pile of photos she had taken at the church and printed earlier. She'd put them there to remind herself to show them to her aunt. Kendra pulled out one of the pine ladderback chairs, sat down, and flipped through the pictures. Looking at the photos taken inside of the church, something flashed through Kendra's mind, but she couldn't make it slow down so she could grab it and identify it.

Boo and Spike decided it was time for breakfast, and twined incessantly around Kendra's ankles then jumped up on the table on the pile of photos. "Grr!" she growled at the cats. "There's something there, but I don't know what it is. I can't grasp it! I hate it when that happens. Don't you?"

Boo sat down and stared at Kendra for a second, then started washing his face. Spike swatted at Boo's tail and they took off together, in a streak of fur.

Kendra shrugged. "Nobody ever listens to me."

She trudged up to her loft, sat down at her computer, and spent the rest of the nighttime hours reading about ghostly apparitions. It was such a comforting nighttime ritual.

CHAPTER THIRTEEN

The next morning, Kendra arrived at Do-Lolly's Diner at the same time her Aunt Jewel did. "You got up early this morning," Kendra called across the parking lot as Jewel climbed out of her old white pickup truck.

"Yeah, I went over to Lila's house to get some iris bulbs she dug up for me."

"That's a score! How did you talk her out of those?" Kendra asked, knowing her aunt had lusted after Lila's purple frilly irises for years.

"Double tangerine daylilies, is how," Aunt Jewel said, and Kendra grinned. She knew the orange daylilies were taking over the side bed on the north side of the house and that Jewel had been trying to give some away for months.

"Now that you've been cleared of the murder, looks like I won't have to start baking cakes with saws in them after all," Kendra said, hugging her aunt. "And look what I got!" She pulled a copy of *Love's Wild Embrace* out of her bag. "Nora called me right after you left this morning and said it had been turned in at the library. I picked it up on my way here."

Aunt Jewel's eyes danced. "I can't wait to read it," she said.

"Oh no, I'm first!" Kendra replied, flipping through the paperback.

"Wait 'til I tell our deputy Jim what you said about the saws," Aunt Jewel answered, grinning.

Kendra laughed. "So he's *our* deputy now, is he? Are you trying to bribe me? You still aren't getting the book first. So, how does it feel to be a free woman?"

"Pretty good, although I always did say I was innocent. What worries me is that the real killer is still loose somewhere here in town."

"Come on, Aunt Jewel. Don't think about that. I'm sure the sheriff and Jim will eventually figure it all out. I'm just glad you're off the hook."

"Did I hear you say that you're off the hook?" Verna Holt called, coming up on the sidewalk behind Aunt Jewel.

"Yes, you heard right. Isn't that wonderful, Verna?"

"Well, uh, of course it is," she said. "It's just that, well, now we still have to worry about the real killer, don't we?"

Aunt Jewel nodded. "That's just what I was saying to Kendra. I'm not too worried, but you can't be too careful, can you?"

"Would you like to join us for breakfast, Mrs. Holt?" Kendra asked.

She backed away, shaking her head. "I'm afraid not. I don't frequent establishments that serve alcohol."

"But it's breakfast; they won't serve beer until later this afternoon. And it's not like it's a honky-tonk, for pete's sake," Aunt Jewel said. "It's a decent family diner."

"No, sorry, I can't do it. If Pastor Holt found out I went in there, he'd never forgive me," she said. "Besides, I have little Honey Bee in the car and I don't want to leave her for very long. I do have the air conditioning on, but she gets so wrought up when I leave her. Sorry, I must run." She turned around and scurried down the sidewalk, turned the corner and was out of sight.

Jewel shook her head. "Wow, she is strict!"

Kendra nodded. "Yeah, tell me about it. Honey Bee, what kind of name is that for a dog?"

They laughed.

When they walked into the diner, Jeremy rushed to give Aunt Jewel a hug and escorted her to her favorite booth. Lolly said that breakfast was on the house and Jeremy rushed to take their orders. Within a few minutes, he was back with steaming hot cups of coffee for everyone.

"So, let's see that book you got this morning," Jewel said.

Kendra flipped it open to the middle and started skimming. After a few moments she fanned herself. "Whoa, this is HOT stuff!"

"Let me see!" Jewel said, snatching the book out of her hands. She opened it to the middle and started reading.

"Wow, this is . . ."

"What?" Kendra asked. "Smut?"

"No! It's pretty good stuff. If you like that sort of thing," Jewel said, blushing.

"Give it back!" Kendra said. She took the book and read the blurb on the back cover. Kendra frowned. Somehow, the story line sounded familiar, like something she'd heard around town. It sounded like people she *knew*, stories she'd heard.

"Does this sound familiar to anyone but me?" she asked. "Seems like I've heard it before somewhere."

"Sure you haven't read the book?" Aunt Jewel asked.

Kendra shook her head. "Yeah, I'm sure. I've never seen it before today. It says that it's about a man who has an affair with two women. It's set in a small town . . ."

She glanced at the cover again. "Adora Lake. It's obviously a pseudonym."

"Yes, but for whom?" Jeremy asked.

"That's probably why it sounds familiar. All that small town stuff is what we live everyday," Jewel said. "And to think people put it into books."

Something tickled at the back of Kendra's mind. "Jeremy, what was it you said that Eula-Mae's son was mumbling during the service? Something about a cake?"

He nodded. "Yes, that's right. He said 'Loving a cake.' Maybe he meant Adora Lake? Adoring a cake? Ack, none of it makes sense!"

Jeremy plopped into the booth next to Kendra. "Scootch over, girlfriend. You won't believe what I heard yesterday."

"Something about Mrs. Bunch?"

"You betcha! We know that Mrs. Bunch-of-Trouble was trying to get Nora kicked off the library committee because of her views on book censorship. Apparently, Nora had it out with her a couple of weeks ago, said she'd better watch out, that she wouldn't stand for it."

Nora threatened Mrs. Bunch, too? Has everyone in town threatened her at one time or another? For cryin' out loud! "Who said that?" Kendra asked.

"Lolly did," Jeremy said, nodding.

Ginger and Virginia walked in just then and Kendra waved them over to their booth. Aunt Jewel slid over to make room.

"What's up, guys?" Ginger asked.

"We're celebrating! Aunt Jewel has officially been cleared of the murder," Kendra said.

"That's great news!" Ginger said, reaching over to pick up the paperback. "And what's this? Breakfast reading? Story time?"

Lolly LaRue came over to the table and greeted the women. "I'll be glad when all this hoo-hah about Mrs. Bunch blows over," she said. "Not that it's bad for business, mind you, but geez loueez! Everybody's nervous that somebody else

141

will get killed before it's over."

"I hope that doesn't happen," Kendra said. "The sheriff seems to think that we're safe."

"Lolly, tell them what you told me about Nora," Jeremy said.

"Oh yeah, she and Bunch got into it not long ago. I had to referee. It was a lot of fun."

"What was it about?" Jewel asked.

"I never found out, and I didn't really care. I just wanted them to leave," Lolly said.

"I'm sorry I wasn't working that day," Jeremy whined.

"You know what else I heard?" Lolly said. "I heard that Nora Rogers and Mrs. Bunch's son—Harry, his name is—they were like this." She entwined her fingers.

"Oh my god," Ginger said, "that man sure got around, didn't he?"

"It's only a rumor, mind you," Lolly said. "But I believe it's true."

"You're saying that they did have an affair?" Kendra asked. "Everybody keeps saying that!"

"Yes ma'am!" Lolly said. "Apparently Mrs. Bunch found out about it and broke it up. He never did get over it, apparently."

"Who told you that?" Aunt Jewel wanted to know.

Lolly shrugged. "I don't even remember who said it. There's been so many in here the last few days talking about it. I heard her funeral sure was strange."

"That's what I heard, too," Virginia said. "What I think's funny is how some of those women dress, like they are still in the 1960s. Hats? Gloves? Geez, that's nutzo."

Aunt Jewel nodded. "It's a whole different world these days, kiddo, but some people are stuck in the past."

"Yeah, I know. I noticed Mrs. Holt always wears those little pillbug hats," Virginia said.

"Sweetie!" Jeremy laughed. "It's *pillbox* hats. I have to say, though, I'd love to get into her closet and root around for a while."

"Speaking of clothes," Ginger said, "we're going shopping for a nice party dress for the high school dance next week. You want to come, Kendra?"

"Nah, y'all go by yourself. Shopping for clothes is always so depressing. It makes me itch."

Ginger looked at Virginia. "Personally I think you should wear your white blouse and navy skirt. You always look nice in that."

Virginia frowned. "Mom! NOBODY wears navy in the summer unless they have to. It's so uncool!"

Jeremy laughed. "She's right, *mother*, it's just not done!"

Ginger nodded. "OK, OK! Then I guess we're going shopping."

Kendra picked up the paperback and skimmed a few more pages. She flipped to the back cover, then inside the last few pages. "Ah! Here it is," she said, " . . . the info on the authors. It says they live 'near Austin' and are a husband and wife team using a pseudonym!"

Suddenly, she remembered where she'd heard the dialogue from the book—in the church! She'd heard Pastor Holt and Verna Holt reciting the lines from the book. Or reading the lines. Or something. What possible reason could they have for doing that? What the hell was going on with those two? Surely the Holts weren't the anonymous authors?

CHAPTER FOURTEEN

Kendra dropped Aunt Jewel back at home then went back downtown to Buddy's Hardware Store & Sundry Sundries to replace the hammer the sheriff had taken as evidence in Mrs. Bunch's murder. As she walked in, Pastor Holt rushed out, almost knocking her down. He mumbled a short hello then raced off down the sidewalk.

"What was that about?" she asked Buddy Byers. "He was in an awful hurry to get out of here."

Buddy was a tall man with a shaved head. He wore two earrings and his arms and neck were covered with tattoos. Kendra wondered when he'd start on his head.

"I have no idea. He's crazy as a bedbug. All I know is that he just paid his account, in full. With cash, too!"

"Did he owe a lot?" Kendra asked.

Buddy nodded. "Yeah, I'll say he did. He owed for over $10,000 worth of building supplies he bought to make repairs on the church building."

"I thought they were broke?"

Buddy shrugged. "They were. But, all of a sudden, the Holts have a boat-load of money. Have you seen that new car of hers?" He whistled. "Man, that's a beaut!"

"Hmm. Any idea where they got the money?" Kendra asked.

Buddy shook his head. "I don't have a clue. All he said was that their ship finally came in and that they were catching up on some bills. I didn't think to ask him what he meant. It's not really any of my business anyway. I'm just glad the bill's paid." He thought a minute. "Come to think of it, maybe I'd better check it to make sure it's not counterfeit. Maybe the good pastor's printing money down in the church basement. Wouldn't that be a hoot?" He laughed then slapped himself on the thigh and went back to work.

Kendra chose a hammer from the dizzying display of choices, paid for it and headed back home. She thought about what Buddy had said. Printing money in the church basement? Surely not. It would explain the extra income, but not the other weirdness going on with those two.

Jewel was in the garden when Kendra got back home. She was digging holes for the irises and had dug up some of the daylilies and put them in a brown paper sack for her friend. "These damned mosquitoes are about to carry me away," she said, swatting at her hair.

146

"I'll put some more of those mosquito dunky thingies in the rain barrels," Kendra said. "That will probably help."

Jewel straightened up, clutching at her back. "I tried to scrub some of that indigo off the bricks, but it's soaked in. I'm afraid we'll have to wait for it to fade. Either that, or replace the bricks."

Kendra walked over to the spot where the murder had taken place. The sheriff had finally removed the crime scene tape. She could see where the bricks were stained. The blood had also soaked in, although it wasn't nearly as noticeable as the indigo blue.

Jewel walked over and stared at the spot. "After all that work putting in the walkway, too. It's a shame."

Kendra stared at her.

"I mean, it's a shame that she's dead, but, well, you know," Jewel finished nervously.

"Yeah, I know," Kendra said. She thought back to the day of the workshop and tried to replay the events in her mind. It was so confusing with so many people milling around, she couldn't remember where anyone was at any point in time.

A brown car pulled up to the curb beside the back fence. The sheriff sat there for a moment, staring at something, then slowly got out of the car, hitched his pants, adjusted his hat.

"Aunt Jewel," Kendra said. "Looks like we have company."

147

"Shit," Jewel said, under her breath. "Wonder what he wants this time?"

He tipped his hat to the women. "Jewel. Kendra. Nice day for gardening, ain't it?"

"No, it's not," Jewel answered. "It's too hot and these danged bloodsuckers are about to do me in. Cut to the chase, Buster. What is it this time?"

He frowned at Jewel then peered at Kendra. "I hear you've been snooping around the church late at night."

She shrugged. "I was there, but I wasn't snooping. Did the Holts file a complaint? I was just taking some photos. For inspiration. I told the Holts that's what I was doing. I'm working on a collection of ghost stories and thought it might help when I get stuck. And I thought I might be able to use some of them for my book cover and on my blog."

He stared at her, squinting. "I see. Good thing, cause I'd hate to think you were trying to solve this murder. You leave the Holts alone. They didn't file a complaint, but they could easily do so. People lurking around there late at night makes them nervous."

Kendra nodded. "I understand." Although she had no intention of staying away if she needed to get more photos.

The sheriff twirled his hat between his hands. "I've talked to everybody who was here during the murder, and I've got it in hand, don't you worry about that. I don't need help from anybody who thinks they're the next Miss Marple. You got that?"

She shrugged. "I'm not trying to solve a murder. That's your job, right?"

He smirked. "That's right, and don't you forget it. But if you DO happen to find the killer, let me know, won't you? I'd appreciate it." He sauntered off, clapping his hat on his head.

"Yikes," Kendra said. "That man's scary."

Jewel smiled. "Yes, he can be. And he's a smart ass," she said. "But a handsome smart ass."

"What?" Kendra asked, staring at her aunt.

Jewel blushed. "Oh, mind your own business. By the way, about what he said—you aren't trying to solve a murder, are you?" Jewel closely watched the sheriff as he climbed into his car and drove away.

Kendra shook her head. "No ma'am, not me."

Jewel gave her an amused look and turned back to her flower bulbs.

Kendra went inside, sat down to work and flipped through the cemetery photos again. There was one amazing tombstone with a tiny lamb sculpture on top, but the photo was too blurry. Too bad, otherwise she'd use it on the cover of her book. She could do a lot with her imaging software, but couldn't fix blurry. She grabbed her camera, decided to go back to the cemetery and take a few more quick shots. And if she had the opportunity, maybe do a little snooping? No,

149

definitely not. She'd promised her Aunt Jewel and the sheriff.

She yelled to her aunt on the way out, said she'd be back in a little while.

It only took ten minutes to get to the churchyard from Kendra's house. A few lights were on in the sanctuary, and the yellow Mercedes wasn't anywhere to be seen.

Kendra entered the church through the front door. It was always left open since so many of the local women came and went, cleaning, changing out the floral arrangements, etc. Luckily, the church office was also unlocked. The desk, however, was not.

Using a letter opener, Kendra finally got the desk drawers open. She rifled through them, and at the bottom, hit pay dirt. A stack of manuscript pages were stacked face down. As she flipped through them, it was obvious it wasn't Pastor Holt's upcoming Sunday sermon. "Adora Lake," she whispered. "Found ya."

She heard a car pull up, doors slammed, then footsteps crunched over the gravel. Kendra quickly grabbed some of the pages and stuffed them down the front of her shirt, and was just turning to leave when the lights flipped on, momentarily blinding her.

When her vision cleared, Kendra saw Verna

Holt standing there with a gun, pointed right at her.

"What the hell are you doing here? Didn't I tell you that we don't want people wandering around here alone? This office is private." Verna waved the gun.

"It was unlocked," Kendra said.

Verna looked at the open desk drawer. "And I assume that was unlocked, too? I told you to mind your own business, didn't I?"

Kendra nodded. "Yes, you did. But there are just a few things I'd like to get straight. There's a rumor going around that you had an affair with Harry, Eula-Mae's son."

Verna blanched, and looked down at the floor. "Where did you hear that? Who said that?"

Kendra shrugged. "You know how things are in this town. Nothing stays hidden for long."

"Awfully nosy, aren't you! So, what if I did?" Verna shrugged. "How is that any concern of yours?"

"And Eula-Mae found out about it, didn't she?" Kendra continued. "I expect, knowing how she was, that she threatened to tell your husband and blow your little secret sky high." Kendra shook her head. "The pastor's wife, of all people."

Verna stared at Kendra. "I've been forgiven for those sins. God has forgiven me."

"Maybe, but Eula-Mae didn't forgive you, did she? Her son turned into a drunk after you were done with him."

151

"I couldn't help that. It wasn't my fault he started drinking and lost his job. I tried to help him. For God's sake, I was in love with the man. But some people just can't be helped."

Just then, Garvey Holt walked in. "I thought I heard voices," he started, then saw the gun in his wife's hand. "For God's sake, Verna, what in the HELL are you doing? Put that down!"

She stared down at the gun then threw it on the desk. "I don't know! Everything's falling apart, I can't think straight. It wasn't supposed to be this way. I can't shoot anybody!"

"No, but you can certainly bash them in the head with a hammer, can't you?" Kendra asked.

Pastor Holt stared at his wife. "What is she talking about?"

Kendra nodded to the pastor. "Did you know about the affair? She says you've forgiven her."

He shook his head. "With Harry Bunch? Yes, I knew about that one. At first I thought it was a tale she was telling. She loves her little stories, you know? I thought it was just one of her sordid tales of love gone wrong that she was spinning for one of her books."

Kendra nodded. "So she's Adora Lake."

"Yes, she writes romances. Well, actually, *we* write them now—romance thrillers for a little extra money. Our writing income over the last two years has kept this church afloat. We're finally making enough money to pay some of our bills."

152

"You're paying the church bills with your book sales?"

He nodded. "That's right."

"So both of you are Adora Lake?"

He nodded. "Nothing wrong with that, is there?"

Kendra shrugged and shook her head. "No, absolutely not. But there is something wrong with murder."

"Murder?" he asked.

"Ask your wife. I thought she murdered Eula-Mae Bunch to shut her up, to keep her from telling you about the affair she had with Harry. She bashed Eula-Mae Bunch over the head with the jar of indigo, and when that didn't kill her, she picked up that hammer and killed her with it. But if you already knew about the affair, then why?" That was the last part of the whole mess Kendra hadn't figured out yet.

Verna stared at Kendra. "Like he just said, my husband already knew about it. But Eula-Mae was going to get right up in front of the whole church and tell them everything—about the affair, about the confessions, about the books. Just when we were finally making it, when some money was starting to come in from our writing, that Bunch bitch had to stick her big nose into our business and ruin it for us."

The pastor stared at Kendra. "I'm sorry y'all got caught up in this, but my wife, well, she wasn't thinking straight. She told me she'd handle the situation. I didn't know she planned to kill the woman." He turned to his wife. "Is this true? DID you kill her? I thought you were going to reason with her, maybe beg her to keep her mouth shut. But murder?"

"I'm sorry!" she cried. "I did it for us. I knew if the rumors got out, then you'd never forgive me. It would ruin what we have here. We couldn't afford for that to happen."

"And what about my camera?" Kendra asked. "It went missing, and I thought I was going nuts. Then I remembered the last time I had it, I was here, at the church. I left it alone in my truck." She stared at Verna. "You took it, didn't you? Then you returned it to my house that day you pretended to come check on Aunt Jewel. What did you do, try to delete the photos?"

Verna smirked. "You tell me, you're so damned smart. Always taking photos, being places you don't have a right to be."

Kendra nodded. "Look at her hands, pastor," she said. "If my suspicions are correct, I think you'll have your answer."

He came over and stood in front of her. "Take off your gloves, Verna. Now."

She hesitated, then did as he asked. Her hands were shaking, and were splotched with dark blue. Verna stared at her husband.

"You told me you spilled some of the dye on your hands during the workshop," he said. "Did you lie to me? Answer me!"

Verna looked down and slowly nodded.

"Dammit, Verna! You had to go mess up the whole plan, didn't you?" The pastor scooped the gun off the desk and waved it at Kendra. "I don't know what I'm going to do about this, but I need time to think about it." He paced back and forth, running his hand through his hair. Finally, he decided. "Come with us."

While Mrs. Holt held the gun, Pastor Holt rummaged around the supply closet until he found a roll of tape. "Sit down!" he ordered, indicating a hard wooden chair in the corner.

Kendra reluctantly sat down and he bound her to the chair. He taped her mouth shut, leaving her nose free so she could breathe.

"Don't worry, somebody will find you eventually. By then, we'll be long gone from here."

She squirmed and tried to yell, but the tape was too tight.

"I do hope you'll forgive us, Kendra," Mrs. Holt said. "This was never supposed to get out of hand like this."

"Come on Verna, we need to get out of here," her husband demanded.

"We have to stop at the house!" Verna squealed.

"What? Why? What are you talking about?"

155

"We have to get Honey Bee! We can't leave her alone there," Verna sobbed.

"Oh, for cryin' out loud, come on then! Damned dog, always causing trouble!" he said, pushing her out the door.

Giving Kendra a backwards glance, they ran out of the office and soon she heard a car-door slam and the engine roar to life. She struggled for a moment, but gave up. Her bonds were just too tight.

"Where in the hell could that girl be at this hour of the night?" Jeremy asked.

Ginger shook her head. "Jewel said she left for the cemetery hours ago. She should be home by now."

She drove around the corner of the church just in time to see the yellow Mercedes peel out of the driveway with the headlights off, in a cloud of dust, gravel flying. The car almost ran head-on into Jewel's truck as they scraped by each other in the narrow driveway.

"Whoa, that's the Holts—wonder why they're in such a hurry?" Jeremy said. "Look! And there's Kendra's car!"

Ginger slammed on the brakes and they jumped out and ran inside. While she searched the sanctuary, Jeremy ran down the hallway to the office. "She's in here!" he called.

156

"Oh, my god, are you OK?" Jeremy grabbed the scissors off the desk and cut the tape off her wrists and gently removed the tape from her mouth.

Ginger pressed a button on her phone. "I'm calling the sheriff."

"Good idea," Kendra agreed, rubbing her wrists. "Cause I have a doozy of a story to tell him, and he's not going to believe it."

CHAPTER FIFTEEN

The group huddled around a large circular booth at Do-Lolly's Diner, enjoying giant hamburgers, fries and pecan pie with coffee.

Lolly came over to refill their cups. "I'm just glad you're OK!" she said, leaning down to give Kendra a one-armed hug.

"Thanks, me too! I'm just glad I have good friends who worry about me," Kendra said.

"And thank goodness the Holts had to go back to their house to get that little dog. Otherwise they might be long gone from here by now," Jewel said.

Just then, Sheriff Buster Briggs walked in and all talking ceased. He looked around, then walked over to their booth. "Evening, everybody," he said, tipping his hat. "Kendra. I just hope you've got the crime solving bug out of your system."

"Yessir, I have," she said, and Jeremy winked at her.

He turned and smiled at Jewel. "Hello, Jewel, how you doin'?"

"Much better now that all of this insanity is behind us," she said, smiling. "Would you like to join us, maybe have a cup of coffee?"

"Nah, I gotta get back to work. I tell you

what, things are busy out there! Y'all enjoy your dinner," he drawled, nodded and turned to go. He hesitated then turned back to Jewel. "You take care of yourself, you hear?" he said, clapped his hat back on his head and sauntered out the door.

"What's THAT all about?" Jeremy asked. "Not that I'm being nosy or anything. So SPILL IT, lady!"

Jewel laughed. "Right, not that you would EVER be nosy."

"Honestly," Jeremy said. "That man was absolutely *twinkling*!"

She shrugged. "We got kinda close these last few weeks while y'all were out sleuthing around. What can I say, he likes my pies."

They all laughed.

"So what tipped you off, Kendra? How did you know what was going on?" Ginger asked.

Kendra shrugged. "Lots of little things, but mostly it was the gloves Verna always wore. At the dye workshop, she said she only had *one* pair, the white ones. And I noticed they were frayed around the cuff, like she'd worn them for a long time. Then, several times after that, she wore blue ones, and they were also frayed around the cuffs. I started thinking about that. She said they'd dyed the old choir robes to keep them nice looking. I started thinking about the blue dye. What if she killed Mrs. Bunch, got the indigo dye on her gloves, then decided to cover it up by dyeing them

159

with the same blue dyes she used for the robes? She kept bragging about how easy it was to use them."

"Wow, that's impressive!" Jeremy said. "She was just persnickety enough to feel that she had to wear gloves, but knew she couldn't wear the white ones with the blue stains on them."

Aunt Jewel shook her head. "I never notice things like that."

Kendra smiled. "Well, I probably wouldn't have either, if Virginia hadn't made that crack about nobody wearing navy in the summer. Mrs. Holt felt like she had to wear gloves, and would rather wear the navy ones than none at all. And, of course, they covered up the stains on her hands she got when she smashed the jar of indigo over Eula-Mae's head."

She turned and smiled at Virginia and they high-fived over the table.

"Well, I DO read Sherlock Holmes," Virginia said. "It's elementary."

"If I ever get that persnickety about my clothing, Kendra, just shoot me," Aunt Jewel said. "Or if I ever start wearing gloves."

Jeremy glanced over and quirked an eyebrow. Jewel was wearing an old pair of jeans, red sandals and a tee-shirt that said *Willie for President.* "I wouldn't worry about that happening anytime soon, sweetie."

Kendra took a sip of her coffee, smiled and

continued. "In those photos I took that first time at the church, I noticed that she was wearing gloves then—dark blue gloves. We know from experience that it's very hard to remove indigo once it gets on your hands. I wondered what she was trying to cover up—why she was wearing the gloves."

Ginger frowned. "I don't understand all of this. OK, so now we know *who* killed her, but *why* did she kill Mrs. Bunch?"

"I wondered about that, too," Kendra said. "But that night I caught them in the office saying those strange things to each other, caught in a compromising position, I wondered if maybe somebody else had seen them there, too. I'll bet Mrs. Bunch also caught them using the office for their writing, and threatened to blackmail them. She's up at the church almost more than anyone else, snooping around."

"Not only were they using church equipment, but also using confessions from the members to inspire their steamy stories," Jeremy said.

"Now that's just trashy!" Virginia said, shaking her head.

"But is that so bad, being inspired by true events?" Ginger asked.

"Maybe not a crime, but Pastor Holt was taking confessions of his congregation and turning them into fiction. That stuff is supposed to be private, sacred, right? After he found out his wife was writing her 'little stories' as he calls them, he

161

decided to help her by spicing them up with some true-to-life tales."

"And perhaps include a few personal experiences in one of them?"

"That's not a crime, either," Jewel said.

"Maybe it's not a crime, but that doesn't make it right," Ginger said.

"Ask me," Jeremy said, "the real issue is the scandal it would cause if people in their church found out. If their congregation found out they were doing that, they'd be out of a job, probably forever. No church would ever hire them again."

"You're probably right about that," Kendra said.

"Pastor Holt told the deputy that he was almost ready to confess when his wife told him that she'd handle the situation. He really didn't know what she was planning to do."

"She handled it all right, by bashing Mrs. Bunch over the head with the indigo jar. When that didn't kill her, she picked up the hammer and finished her off. Maybe she got angry and picked up the indigo, but using the hammer was pure murder."

Aunt Jewel cringed. "What a messy business! And right in our own garden, too."

"You got that right," Kendra said. "Of course, small town drama is always a messy business."

"We excel in messy business here in Nameless," Jeremy agreed. "Maybe I should write a play about it. I'll need costumes! I wonder what I would have to do to get a look inside Verna Holt's closet?"

"I wonder if all that will end up in another Adora Lake book someday," Ginger said. "It would make a great juicy murder mystery. After all, prisoners write novels all the time."

"Speaking of books," Aunt Jewel said, "Kendra, you and me, we could write one of those steamy novels and make us some money."

"Yes!" Jeremy said, clapping his hands. "I love that! You could call it *Nameless Desires*! Let me help!"

"Or how about *Naughty in Nameless*?" Ginger suggested.

Virginia said, "I'll bet I can top those. I like mom's idea about a murder mystery. Let's see . . . how about *A Deep Blue Indigo Death*? It could be about a dye workshop that goes kerflooey!"

Kendra laughed. "I think I'll stick to writing articles about UFOs, chupacabras and ghost stories. They may not pay as much, but they seem *much* safer to me." She grinned at her aunt. "But you know what? You should go for it. Seriously."

Aunt Jewel smiled mysteriously. "Maybe I will, at that. Maybe I will."

THE END

Note from the Author

Thanks so much for reading DYE, DYEING, DEAD. I appreciate your support of my writing. I hope you enjoyed it. Won't you please take a moment to leave a review for the book online at your favorite book retailer?

ABOUT THE AUTHOR

Bobbi A. Chukran is the author of LONE STAR DEATH and the "Nameless, Texas" mystery series, as well as other award-winning comedy plays and best-selling short stories.

Bobbi A. Chukran is a multi-generational Texan, born in Ft. Worth. She has "small town" in her blood and loves writing about quirky characters and strange happenings. She was raised in a small town, educated in a big town and went back to small-town living as soon as possible. Now she lives in Taylor, a small town right outside Austin. She and her husband, Rudy, spend time remodeling, herding cats and tending a large garden. He plays the guitar while she writes and curses things like hyperlinks.

Bobbi blogs about writing, her inspiration for the stories and more at:

http://bobbichukran.blogspot.com

For more information, please check out her website:

http://bobbichukran.com

Other Books by Bobbi A. Chukran
LONE STAR DEATH
PRINCESS PRIMROSE & the CURSE OF THE
     BIG SLEEP
THE JOURNAL OF MINA HARKER
CATTYWAMPUS CHRISTMAS (coming in
     December 2014)

**Other Short Stories in the "Nameless, TX"
Series:**
Aunt Jewel and the Purloined Pork Loin
Aunt Jewel and the Poisoned Potlikker
Dewey Laudermilk and the Peckerwood Tree
Best Halloween Ever, 1965

Amazon Author Page:
http://www.amazon.com/Bobbi-A.-
Chukran/e/B005UK1P7M

Friend me on Facebook:
https://www.facebook.com/bobbichukranauthor

Follow me on Twitter:
https://twitter.com/bchukran

Pinterest:
http://www.pinterest.com/bobbichukran/

E-book versions of DYE, DYEING, DEAD are also available.

INSPIRATION FOR THE BOOK

Over 20-years ago, I started a mystery series featuring a weaver sleuth. The first book was called DEEP BLUE INDIGO DEATH. Things happened, I got busy with other projects, and the book was set aside. I wrote other things, mostly non-fiction garden and craft books. One of my books, COLORS FROM NATURE, was on natural dyeing. In the process of writing that book, I made my own "vat" of indigo in a two-gallon jar. I maintained it for years, carrying it around with me as we moved from house to house. I grew a huge dye plant garden that included indigo, madder, coreopsis, marigolds, rosemary and more.

I eventually started writing more fiction and kept thinking about the weaver sleuth and the possibility of using indigo in the plot. I wondered, what if a murder takes place during a dye workshop? Years passed and I started my Nameless, Texas short story series. When I decided to write a longer book introducing that series, I remembered the dyeing book sitting on my hard drive. I resurrected it, changed the name of the town from No-Name to Nameless and changed the sleuth's name from Kendra O'Keefe to Kendra Louise Harper.

167

Another thing that changed was her occupation. I wanted Kendra to have a slightly different focus. Since I'm an avid reader of Texas lore and folklore, and all things strange, I decided to make Kendra an independent folklorist and author. That way, she can investigate things like ghosts, UFOs, chupacabras, legends about plants—and natural dyeing.

Kendra's aunt, Jewel Moore, is the avid gardener in the stories. Since I'm also a gardener who lives in a vintage house like Kendra and Jewel, the series incorporates many of my personal interests. And of course, they have cats. Right now, I tend six indoor rescue cats and feed additional ferals.

I hope you'll enjoy the stories and books set in the small Texas town of Nameless.

And how did I name the town? I used to live in Leander, Texas. Back in the 1880s, it was called Nameless because the city officials couldn't decide on a name. I lived on Nameless Road. After moving away from there, I decided to honor the name of the original town where the story was first conceived by using it for my series.

Happy trails to you, until we meet again!

Bobbi A. Chukran